# An Angel's Secret

# An Angel's Secret

A Thurston Hotel Novel
Book Ten

Ellen Jorgy

www.ellenjorgy.com
Facebook @ellenjorg2

ISBN 978-0-9953035-1-5

Publisher: Ellen Jorgensen
Cover Design: Su Kopil

**www.ellenjorgy.com**

# Dear Reader

When Brenda Sinclair shared her idea of writing a series of books featuring The Thurston Hotel, and set in the fictional town of Harmony, Alberta, I had mixed feelings. I have spent years dreaming about writing, and thinking about writing, and have even done some writing, but to actually publish? And with a time deadline? That is scary stuff, I can tell you.

Being a perfectionist at heart, I want my writing to be perfect, yet nothing ever is, and if you wait for perfection, you will never actually do anything. So, with some trepidation, I hitched myself up to Brenda's series. Looking back now, I'm so glad I did.

Thank you to Brenda and all the other Thurston authors for blending your stories with mine, for cooperating with weather, and geographic features, and hotel uniforms, and everything else we had to agree upon. You ladies are my tribe. I salute you all.

A huge thank you goes out to Bob, Abby, and Eric, who put up with mommy being "busy" while appearing to be doing nothing more than sitting in front of a computer and staring off into space for long periods of time. I promise I'll make better suppers until I start the next novel.

To you, my readers, I hope this story makes you laugh, cry, hold your breath, and keep reading well past your bed time. If I can do any of those things I will consider this a tremendous success.

Happy reading!

# Acknowledgments

Thank you to Brenda Sinclair for allowing me to participate in this project. It has been a tremendous experience.

Thank you to Brenda, Victoria Chatham, and Suzanne Stengl, for your editing input. I appreciate every comment and suggestion offered.

A special thank you to the very talented Su Kopil from Earthy Charms Designs for crafting my beautiful cover. I absolutely adore it. Please check out her website at www.earthlycharms.com to view her designs.

Thank you to Ted Williams for the most precise and detailed line editing. You made me look like a pro, you clever man!

Thank you to all the other authors who worked together so well to help create the wonderful town of Harmony, Alberta, and it's many interesting citizens. May the lights flicker, and the faint scent of tobacco follow you, wherever you go.

# Dedication

To Bob,
Your love and support made this happen.

# Chapter One

Like an avenging angel, the bicyclist flew down the trail, heading straight for the dog. Tessa Peters watched helplessly as her young German Shepherd, Otis, stood frozen on the path.

"Otis, come!" Tessa yelled.

At the last second, the dog leapt out of the way as the bicyclist skidded to a halt in a cloud of dust. The man swung his leg over the bike, crouched down, and whistled softly to Otis.

"Otis, come!" she tried again.

Otis didn't come. Instead, with head low and tail wagging, he trotted over to the man.

Tessa clenched her teeth and fisted her hands. Stupid men. They should all be shot. First she had to deal with the drunken idiots on the late shift, and now this, this . . . This fool!

"Hey, buddy," she yelled, striding toward the man. "You almost hit him!"

The guy stood up. And up. He was so tall. At least six foot or more. And, damn if he wasn't smiling at her as she approached.

Tessa almost swallowed her own tongue. Wow! He sure didn't look like an idiot or a fool.

She couldn't help but stare. He was the last thing she'd expected to see on this late September afternoon. His blue performance T-shirt stretched tautly across a broad chest. Black bike shorts fit like a second skin over well-muscled legs. Her eyes darted down and back up, hesitating over his gorgeous row of white teeth, and finally locking onto his deep blue-gray eyes.

What had she planned to yell at him?

"Sorry about that." His smile widened. "I know it looked like I was going too fast, but I saw this handsome fellow way back. I wasn't going to run into him. My name's Luke."

Tessa stared, momentarily confused when he offered his hand to her. Shake hands, Tess. Don't act like a nit. You've seen men before. He's no different. She smiled back and took his hand. A warm flush swept up her arm leaving her feeling breathless. "Tessa Peters," she mumbled.

"Nice to meet you, Tessa." Luke took off his riding helmet and crouched down to the dog again. Otis sat, tongue lolling out, seeming to grin from ear to ear. Tessa couldn't help noticing Luke's caramel gold hair was almost the same shade as the golden tan markings of the dog.

"How old is he?" Luke resumed the ear scratching with both hands.

"Just over a year," Tessa replied.

"What are you training? The usual stuff?"

"Well, that and a bit more. I'm training him to track a scent. I'd like to be able to use him to help with the local search and rescue team. I volunteer when I can."

"Cool," he replied. "So you like the outdoors then?"

"Love it," she answered, and almost melted when he grinned up at her. Dimples. Two of them! And his hair was all damp and wavy from being in the helmet. It should be illegal to look that hot. She cleared her throat nervously. "And you? I mean, you obviously like biking," she inquired, lamely.

* * *

"That and hiking. In the summer I mean. I ski in the winter, and snowshoe. And I like dogs." Luke stood up mentally groaning. *And I like dogs.* Good Lord, he hadn't sounded that awkward since junior high. What was wrong with him?

One more look at the pretty, fresh-faced blonde with a ponytail was all the answer he needed. Who could possibly sound sophisticated with such a little bombshell looking at him? She barely came to his shoulder, and her hazel eyes were now peeping up at him from under her lashes. His heart raced, and it wasn't just from the five kilometer mountainous descent.

"I'm surprised I haven't seen you around before," she said.

"I've only been in town a month," he replied. "I've been pretty busy, settling in. But I have been able to ride the trails a fair bit. Do you ride?" He found himself holding his breath.

"Yes, some. I'm probably not as fast as you though."

"For you, I'd slow down any time." He watched pink creep into her cheeks. She was absolutely adorable.

They stared at each other a moment. She was fidgeting with her fingers and shuffling her feet a bit. Could she feel as nervous as he did?

"I, uh, guess I should get going. I need to get Otis home and feed him," she said finally. "I have an early morning tomorrow."

"Oh, sure." Luke bent down to retrieve his helmet and bike. He didn't want this conversation to end so soon. He started walking his bike to his old Toyota pick-up. His heart pounded. He spun around and called,

"What are you doing Friday night? Would you like to grab dinner with me?"

She turned toward him but he couldn't read her expression.

"I have a thing Friday."

Was that disappointment in her voice? He wasn't sure.

"I'm going to train Otis again Saturday. Maybe you'd like to help?"

"I'd love to." Yes! He tried to sound casual. "What time?"

"Meet me here about one? Have you seen Harmony Falls yet? We could hike up there afterwards. It's not far."

"That sounds nice." He smiled. "One o'clock it is."

He stood, helmet clasped in his hands, as she clipped the leash to Otis' collar. She turned away but glanced over her shoulder with a smile before heading toward a dilapidated Volkswagen Beetle in the parking lot. She unlocked the door and ordered the big Shepherd into the back seat, then waved before climbing in herself.

Luke watched as her little bug disappeared down the dusty gravel road to town. He was surprised the thing had started. It looked in pretty rough shape, even worse than his junker truck.

He grabbed his bike and hefted it easily into the back of the pick-up. The bike, with its ultralight aluminum frame and wheels with knobby tires, was just the thing for tackling the trails in Alberta's Rocky Mountains. At just under ten grand, it had cost more than his truck by about double, but was worth every penny. The truck, however, was just to get from point A to point B and he didn't care if it was fancy or not, as long as it worked.

* * *

Tessa drove down the road. Otis was technically in the back seat, but he positioned himself in the middle, and was so large his head and chest occupied the front of the car. He sat panting in her ear and looking out the front window like a co-pilot.

She couldn't seem to wipe the grin from her face. Truth be told, she didn't have time for a relationship. It could only complicate things, and she sure didn't want to end up like her mom.

Why had she agreed to this? Maybe because Luke seemed different somehow. She'd felt hopeful looking into those sea blue eyes. Besides, Otis was ready for his next phase of training and for that she needed a partner. So really, this was for Otis' benefit.

Oh, who was she kidding? Luke was absolutely delicious!

She sighed as she weaved down the winding road toward town. From up here the little town of Harmony, Alberta, sat nestled in the mountains, their steep rocky slopes cradling it like a bowl, creating a perfect place for skiers, hikers and nature lovers to find a touch of comfort. She could see the town hall and the Thurston Hotel where she worked. The little creek that passed behind the hotel glittered in the sun like a string of diamonds.

She'd thought Harmony was going to be her little safe haven from the mean old world outside, but trouble liked to follow her. Would Luke prove to be more trouble in her messed up world?

"I guess we'll see, won't we, Otis?"

# Chapter Two

Tessa awoke with a start. Flailing blindly in the dark, it took her three tries to hit the alarm and turn it off. She slumped back on her pillow, blinking owlishly. After a moment, she forced herself into a sitting position and flicked on the light. She hated taking a nap in the evening, it was so hard to get going again, but if she didn't she'd never make it through the late shift.

'The late shift'. That's what she called it. She didn't like calling it what it was. Some people wouldn't mind. Some people actually enjoyed it, or so they claimed. Tessa didn't. It felt odd, uncomfortable. This wasn't her. Not really.

'Necessity is the mother of invention.' That's what old Mrs. Arbuckle at the hotel had said to her. There surely was a big necessity in her life and so she had invented a solution. So what if it felt like stuffing your foot into a shoe that was too small. It got the job done and that was all that mattered.

Tessa climbed out of bed and scuffed to the bathroom of her small basement suite. She showered quickly, toweled off and loaded her damp blonde hair with volumizing mousse. Ten minutes blow drying upside down had her hair puffed and dry.

"What are you looking at, dog?" she asked Otis. "Don't give me that look. I don't need the face from you as well as from my mom." The big German Shepherd swished his tail back and forth across the floor, panting. "Come on. Outside with you. You can get some fresh air until I get home."

Tessa grabbed her garment bag and let them both outside. She gave Otis a gentle stroke on his head before leaving the backyard and locking the gate securely behind her. She threw her bag into the old Volkswagen Beetle, and climbed in.

The Wobbly Dog was only twelve blocks down the road from her house. In the summer she rode her bike there. But autumn in the mountains meant the sun had set three hours ago and the air had an icy chill to it. So Tessa drove and had to circle the block around the pub three times before she found someone leaving and took their spot.

She knocked loudly at the back entrance of the pub. The door cracked open and a very white eyeball in a dark, bald head assessed her briefly.

"You late." The door opened fully to admit her.

"I'm not late. I still have forty-five minutes."

"You girls be takin' longer than forty-five minutes, fo' sure," Big Joe rumbled softly. "You best to be hurryin'."

"I'll be ready, Jo-Jo. You just keep people off the stage. No grabbing."

"That fo' sure. No problem, Miss Tess. No one touch you like that while I be here."

Tessa left the large Jamaican bouncer with his shiny bald head at the rear door and hurried to the change room. The other two girls gave no notice that they even saw her as she took her seat at the mirror. Professional jealousy, Tessa guessed. She mentally shrugged. She wasn't here to make friends.

It wasn't her fault she got better tips than they did. Or maybe it was her fault. She certainly worked hard enough. She threw everything she had into this gig, and then some. She deserved those tips. She needed them too. So what if she felt a little nauseous right now. It would pass. It always did, eventually.

Tessa began her transformation. Thick, long black eyelashes were carefully glued in place. Next came contouring to diminish her nose and hollow her cheeks, followed by foundation to cover the freckles. Eyeliner and shadow made her eyes look huge. Her lips were outlined a bit oversize, and filled in with deep red color and shimmery highlights to exaggerate her pout.

She added clip-in blonde extensions to her hair, being careful to conceal them well so they wouldn't show even when she tipped her head upside down. They had been pricey, but they looked so good no one could tell it wasn't all her own hair. After that it took only a couple more minutes to change into her costume.

One final look in the mirror. The exotic beauty with cat-like eyes and a tawny mane of hair staring back at her was barely recognizable. Perfect. Her own grandmother couldn't tell who she was.

"Hello, Misty Dawn. Are you ready to work?" she whispered to the mirror. Misty smiled sadly back at her.

"Hey," Big Joe said from near the stage entrance, "That's yo' cue. Go on now."

"And NOW, the girl you've all come to see: Misty Dawn!" the DJ announced loudly.

The music ramped up. Tessa paused for effect, then pushed through the curtain to a roar of applause.

The music throbbed.

She strutted and twirled.

The frenzy rose.

Her clothes peeled off.

One... piece... at... a... time.

# Chapter Three

Tessa couldn't decide if she was excited or terrified when she saw Luke's old pick-up pull to a stop in the cross-country ski parking lot where she waited. He'd played on her mind for the past two days, distracting her from her work at the hotel, making her forget to clean things. It was maddening! She was so wired that Otis was twitchy too, and lunged forward on his leash, exploding into a frenzy of barking when Luke stepped out.

He walked toward them wearing jeans and an open-collared red plaid shirt over his T-shirt. Tessa thought he looked mighty fine, but Otis acted as if he were the devil incarnate. His teeth clacked together with every bark.

"Halt," she commanded, tugging his collar sharply.

"Hey there, fella. It's me, remember," Luke called out as he approached.

At the sound of Luke's voice, Otis' barking ceased and he began wagging his tail wildly while Tessa fought to keep the big dog under control.

Luke crouched to the ground and was immediately knocked flat on his back by Otis' joyous greeting. "Whoa!" He laughed, fending off dog kisses.

"Otis! Off!" Tessa finally pulled him back. "I'm so sorry. He's still got a puppy brain in that big body."

"Don't worry about it," Luke said, climbing back to his feet and dusting off his backside. "I like him. He sure is big though. How much does he weigh?"

"I think he's about eighty-five pounds now, but he still has some filling out to do. Oh, gosh. Look at your back. You're covered in dirt."

"Want to get that for me? It's hard to reach."

He turned away from her and she couldn't help but notice how broad his shoulders were. She began brushing the dust off. The feel of his back, warm and firm in the autumn sun, gave her all sorts of crazy thoughts which brought a flush to her face.

"There," she offered. "Much better."

"Thanks." Luke smiled and Tessa thought the sun glowed warmer in that moment.

"So what's the plan?" he continued.

"Well, I've trained Otis to follow a track I've laid down with my own scent. He can follow that through a field or through the woods. Now I have to get him trained to follow someone else's scent. He naturally wants to find me, because he loves me, but getting him to follow someone else will be harder. That's where you can help me, if you're up for it."

"Well, I can see why he'd want to follow you." Luke bent to ruffle Otis' fur.

Tessa glanced quickly at him and caught the twinkle in his eye and the half-smile he tried to hide. She felt her face heat and quickly turned back to Otis. Luke was flirting with her, wasn't he? She was almost sure of it, but why? She should be used to getting attention, except she rarely got attention dressed in jeans and a baggy sweatshirt. Tessa didn't get attention as Tessa.

Now Misty Dawn, on the other hand, got lots of attention; rude, lascivious, completely unwanted attention. But she never acknowledged it. She smiled, and nodded, and looked right through them as if they weren't there. It was only fair, because they looked at *her* as if she weren't there. In their eyes she was an object to be looked at, used, but not treated like a person.

"So. How do we do this?"

Luke's question bounced her back to the moment.

"First, we have to go out further in the woods to get away from this high traffic area. There are too many smells here. We have to make it a little easier for him while he's learning. There's a nice meadow I like to start from just up the trail from here."

"Lead on," Luke said.

Otis lead the way, nose hovering just above the ground. Tessa followed holding Otis' long leash, with Luke walking by her side. She glanced up at him again to find him watching her.

"So what do you do when you aren't training Otis? Do you work with the Fire Department?" Luke asked.

"No." She laughed. "I'm just a maid at the Thurston Hotel. I work weekdays from eight until three."

"That hotel is a landmark around here, isn't it?"

"Yes. It was started in 1916 by Thomas Thurston. They just celebrated their one hundred year anniversary this past August. It's a pretty good place to work. The people are nice.

"Okay. Here we are," Tessa announced, changing the subject before he could ask more questions about her activities. "First, do you have anything of yours that I can use for Otis to get a scent from? I should have asked you to bring something but I didn't think of it until this morning and then I didn't have your number."

"Oh. I don't know," Luke said, looking down at himself. He patted his pockets, looking for something. "Not really. I have keys but those don't hold a scent well. Hmm. I know. It's pretty warm today." He started unbuttoning his shirt.

"What are you doing?" Tessa blurted, mildly alarmed. It was too soon in this friendship to be getting undressed.

"I'll just take my T-shirt off and put the flannel one back on," he said with a grin. He dropped the flannel one on the ground and peeled off his T-shirt. Tessa couldn't tear her eyes away as the white shirt pulled up showing off the ripped muscles underneath. She tried to keep her face blank but had to forcibly shut her mouth to keep from gaping.

"Here. This should smell like me." He handed the T-shirt to her and then snatched his flannel from the ground. He gave it a shake before slipping his arms in and doing his buttons back up.

Tessa resisted the urge to smell the shirt herself. Steady girl. Get a grip. Deep breath, and continue.

"I have some special treats here." She pulled a baggie out of her pocket. "He only gets these when he's found me. Today, he has to find *you* to get a treat."

"Here." She handed the bag over to Luke. "I'm going to stay here in the meadow and not let Otis watch you. You walk straight down that path, and when you see the big fallen log go lie down behind it."

"Big fallen log?" Luke asked dubiously.

"Yes. You can't miss it. Just lie down behind it and be very quiet. Otis needs to use his nose not his ears to find you."

"Because a lost person might be hurt and not able to call out," Luke finished. "I get it. Okay. Here goes."

Luke headed out the trail and Tessa turned Otis to face the other way. She made him watch her face to keep his full attention on her and away from Luke. When she felt enough time had passed she turned Otis around and walked him to where she'd left the T-shirt on the ground.

"Suche!" she commanded, pointing to the shirt. The German word for search sounded more like 'zoo-her' and

Otis immediately dropped his nose to the ground and began snuffing at the fabric.

"Suche, Otis. Suche," she repeated. The dog cast back and forth then seemed to settle on a path and began following Luke's route out of the meadow.

Tessa let out his twenty foot lead to give him freedom to follow the trail. Knowing which way Luke had gone helped her correct and aid the young dog as he progressed. The designated log lay not far into the woods and was an easy target for a first attempt at tracking a different person.

As Otis approached where Luke might have veered off the path, he slowed and began casting back and forth.

"Suche, Otis," Tessa encouraged him.

Otis seemed to decide on a path and veered to the right, toward the log. Tessa was thrilled to watch him circle the log and then drop into a down position, his signal that he had found something. He whined softly. She followed him around the log and found Luke, flat on his back, eyes tight shut until one cracked open to peek at her.

"Good boy!" Tessa praised Otis. "Luke, you can give him his treat now."

"Good boy, Otis," Luke said, laughing. He sat up and dug a piece of bacon from his pocket to offer the dog.

Otis leapt up, wagging his whole body, and climbed all over Luke in an effort to get the bacon. Luke flopped back down, grabbing Otis' ruff and wrestling with the big dog for a moment.

"That went well," Luke said. "Want to try it again?"

"Sure. If you don't mind," Tessa answered.

They repeated the process a few more times. Each search was a little farther, and a little more complicated, but Otis succeeded with a few corrections.

"I'm getting cold," Tessa said. "We did more today than I thought we would. We should call it quits."

Luke looked up at the sun just starting to sink behind the mountains. "Yes. We should go back. The parking lot isn't far. I should put my T-shirt back on."

Tessa handed him the shirt. She tried not to stare as he began unbuttoning his flannel — she hated it when men stared at her — but her eyes kept flicking toward him. He saw her look and grinned at her. Tessa felt her face flush and quickly turned to pick up a stick to throw for Otis.

They started back down the trail toward the parking lot, walking in amiable silence. Tessa held Otis' lead and he walked on her left. Luke was on her right, close but not quite touching. She could feel the current between them so strong it almost sparked. He was gorgeous.

Tessa hated the guys who radiated complete superior arrogance as if they thought they were God's gift to womankind. That turned her off faster than a bucket of ice-water over the head. Although more handsome than any man she'd ever met, Luke didn't seem to realize it. He was a complete gentleman. There were no arrogant remarks, no lewd come-ons, only respect and laughter.

She stole a quick glance up at him to find him staring back at her. Their eyes locked for a moment and her breath caught in her chest. She could sink into that ocean blue gaze and be lost forever. She tore her eyes away abruptly, as a tickle of fear ran down her spine. This guy had the power to really hurt her. If she wasn't careful, she'd end up just like her mom.

"I'm starving," Luke said. "Can I buy you dinner?" They stepped into the parking lot and headed toward her car.

"Oh. I wish I could but I have a thing tonight."

"Again?" Luke sounded disappointed.

"Yes. I'm sorry. I work a late shift Friday and Saturday nights. I need to take Otis home and feed him before I go."

"Lunch then? Tomorrow?" he tried again.

Tessa's heart warmed. He sure was persistent. He must actually like her. "Okay. When?"

"I'll pick you up around one. What's your address?"

Tessa told him with a thread of excitement dancing up and down her spine. Or was it trepidation? She wasn't sure, but she couldn't seem to keep her hopes down.

# Chapter Four

"Pastor Luke! You didn't!" Mrs. Delores Reid looked appalled.

"What?" He sounded defensive even to his own ears. Delores was secretary for Winding River Church in Harmony, and as such, technically, she worked for him. She didn't seem to have gotten that memo, however, and she treated him more like a grandson than a boss.

To be honest, he didn't really mind. He'd never known either of his own grandmothers, but if he could have picked one, Delores would have been it. She was stern, disciplined, and in the few short weeks he'd been here, she'd spoiled him rotten. With her softy curled grayish blonde hair and unlined face, he pegged her age as somewhere between fifty and a hundred, but didn't dare ask for clarification.

"Tell me I didn't just hear you say you stripped half-naked in front of that young woman!" she continued, her clear blue eyes seeing right through him.

"It wasn't like *that*. She's training her dog and needed a scent article. I just offered my shirt."

Delores made a small disapproving noise in the back of her throat. "That is not appropriate behavior for the pastor of a church, especially a young one who looks like you."

"What do you mean 'looks like me'? Is there something wrong with the way I look?" Luke glanced down at himself.

She eyed him up and down, then said, "No. That's the problem."

"I like her, Delores. She's different somehow. Special. I can't explain it."

"Humph. All the more reason to keep your shirt on… Well. Tell me about her," Delores prodded.

"Tessa's beautiful! She has the prettiest eyes. Kinda green mixed with gold and brown."

"You mean hazel?" She smiled in a grandmotherly way.

"Yeah. And she doesn't wear any make-up. Just natural, with a few freckles across her nose. And she has a German Shepherd dog. She likes the outdoors, hiking. She's everything you don't find in a city girl," he finished with a grin.

"She sounds lovely. What church does she go to? She doesn't sound like any of the young women who attend here," Delores asked.

Luke looked away briefly and scratched the back of his head. "I, um, don't know if she goes anywhere."

"Then you need to slow down and not get too attached to her until you find out. As pastor of this church any woman you choose to marry becomes not only your life partner but also co-leader of this church. If she doesn't share your faith this will never work out for the long term. Then you will have not only hurt yourself, but her also," Delores cautioned.

"I know. But I feel drawn to her…" Luke trailed off.

"Well, you'd best back off. The church chose you to replace Pastor Carmichael because there are so many youths who need guidance in this community. Many of the congregation thought you were the right man to reach them because of your own experiences. They believe you can lead us forward, but there were others who felt you were too young and inexperienced to be lead pastor. Be careful you don't prove them right. You need a wife, not a fling, Luke. Without faith this girl cannot be for you."

Luke turned away from Delores' piercing gaze. She was right. He knew it, but the old rebellion in him raised its head to resist her wise counsel.

How could what he was feeling not be from God?

He felt so drawn to Tessa, like he'd known her forever. It was as if she had been made especially for him, but perhaps that was just his own wishful thinking. At any rate, he'd already invited her to lunch tomorrow, and he wasn't about to back out. He'd invite her to church next week and see what she'd say.

The phone ringing turned Delores' attention away from him. "Hello. Winding River Church. Delores speaking," she said. "Calm down, dear. I can barely understand you." She frowned. "Yes. Yes. Just a moment and I'll get Pastor Dixon."

She covered the phone with her palm and turned to Luke. "It's Riley Hamilton, the mayor's daughter. She's the young lady who is to be married here come December. She's very upset. You'd best speak to her. Oh, and when you're done, I left a casserole for you in the fridge in the church nursery. You know, in case you didn't have time to cook today."

"Thank you, Delores. You're the best."

She made a noise in the back of her throat again but Luke caught her slight smile and the twinkle in her eye. She handed him the phone and quietly left his office, closing the door gently behind her.

"Riley. This is Pastor Luke. How can I help you?"

# Chapter Five

Tessa swirled around the pole as the music throbbed and the men leered. It was pretty drunk in the bar, as usual. She focused her gaze over everyone's head, trying not to really see anyone in particular. She moved through her routine, making sure to get close to the customers waving money. She thrust out her hip to allow the twenties to be slipped under her tiny G-string. Her barely-there bra was still on and she leaned forward to allow a fifty to be slipped between her cleavage. Someone made a grab for her but she moved aside quickly.

*Damn you, Robbie, this is all your fault.*

In a moment Big Joe had the offender by the scruff of his neck and was talking into his ear. Tessa couldn't hear what was said, but the guy's face drained of color, so obviously Jo-Jo got his point across.

She was almost done her final set when she saw them come through the door. Her stomach clenched. The two big men had come every Saturday since she'd worked here, without fail. They moved to the back of the bar and commandeered two seats from the young men originally sitting there, neither of whom seemed inclined to argue with them.

Tessa waved her farewell from the stage and moved back into the dressing area, in a cold sweat. She quickly gathered all her tips into an envelope and threw on her jeans and a hoodie. She shoved her feet into her sneakers and made her way back out into the bar.

"Mishty Daawn," a very drunk man called out to her. "Want to come home wif me?" He waved twenty bucks at her.

"Go away," she replied, pushing past him and heading toward the enormous men at the back of the room.

"Here," she offered quietly, handing over the envelope. "That's all I've got."

The one named Marco opened the envelope and riffled through the money. "That's it?" He leveled a baleful look at her. "You're short."

"Things have been quiet this week. October is always slow. It'll pick up once ski season starts," she replied breathlessly. She wrapped her warms around herself, keeping her head low.

"You could earn more than this if you come work for us in Calgary. Lots more. Right, Frank?"

Frank nodded solemnly. "Lots more," he rumbled.

Tessa paled. She didn't want to work for them. Not now. Not ever. "N-no thanks. This will get it done. I'll do better next weekend."

"You'd better or you ain't ever gonna get this paid off." He smiled in a way that made her stomach curl.

"Are we done?" she asked sullenly.

Marco and Frank stood up, towering over her.

"Yeah. We're done... 'Til next week," Marco said.

They pushed their way out of the bar leaving Tessa feeling lost and alone in the crowd. She shivered. How had it ever come to this?

"You okay, Miss Tessa?"

The sound of Big Joe's voice right behind her ear made her jump.

"You want for me to throw those two out next time they show up?" he asked. "I do it, no worries."

"No, Jo-Jo. That's okay. We have a business arrangement," Tessa said softly.

"Den why you look scared? I don't like them. Maybe I should call de police next time they come in."

"No. Don't do that." Tessa's voice rose a notch. She shook her hair back and faked a smile for his benefit. She didn't want him to get hurt too. "We just have a little arrangement. It will be fine."

She saw Big Joe's skepticism, but couldn't let him interfere. He could only make things worse than they already were. "Really. It'll be fine. Just leave them be."

"Okay, but I don't like it. If you change your mind I be happy to kick them out." Big Joe scowled fiercely, but she saw the concern in his eyes.

"Thank you, Jo-Jo. I'll keep that in mind. I have to get home now." She pushed her way back through the crowd and disappeared into the changing area. She appreciated his offer, but there was more to it than he understood, and she couldn't put him at risk. He was the one friend she had who knew about Misty Dawn and still liked her.

\* \* \*

Luke wiped his sweaty palms down his jeans and took a deep breath. Easy boy, it's just lunch, no reason to be so nervous. He knocked on the door and heard Otis explode in a fit of barking on the other side. The door cracked open and Tessa peered out. Below her, a huge black nose was trying to force its way through the door to get at him.

"Please say something to this dog so he'll settle down." Tessa laughed, the sound music in his ears.

"Otis. Buddy. Calm down, dude."

The barking stopped and Tessa opened the door to let Otis out. Luke bent down to pet the dog's head and ruffle his fur. "Good boy, Otis! You keep out the bad guys," he teased.

He glanced up when Tessa made a funny little noise. "What'd you say?" he asked. She seemed pale all of a sudden.

"Oh. Nothing." She turned away from him. "I'll just get my purse," she added quickly. "Can you lock Otis in the back yard for me please?"

Her basement suite door was off the side of the house and right beside the gate to a fenced back yard. Luke shooed the dog into the yard and securely latched the gate. Tessa was locking her own door by the time he was done.

"You look great." He watched the pink creep into her cheeks and grinned a little broader.

It was true. Snug jeans showed off the curve of her hip and a soft peach sweater made her skin seem to glow. She was even prettier than he had remembered. Except, now that he looked closer, there seemed a shadow under her eyes, like she was tired. Well, a nice lunch would help that. Food always made him feel better anyway. "Where would you like to eat? I hear the Thurston Hotel has a nice coffee shop," he offered.

When she nodded agreement, Luke led the way to his truck. He went around and opened the door for her just the way Pastor Johnson had taught him. He was rewarded with a surprised look of pleasure from Tessa.

He reached the main doors to the lobby of the Thurston Hotel just ahead of her, and held the big door open for her to pass through. The old hotel had the gracious charm of the era it was built in. The six story, sandstone and brick landmark had just celebrated its one hundredth anniversary. Luke looked over the plush lobby with interest.

"Hi Gill." Tessa smiled at a young bellhop as they passed him in the lobby.

Gill waved back at Tessa, grinning ear to ear. He looked smart and trim in the black with emerald green bellhop's uniform of the Thurston Hotel. Gill still had the gangly walk of a teenager, and managed to trip over a small carry-on bag as he gathered up a pile of luggage to take upstairs.

"I've just got to carry these up to room 31. Then I promised to walk Killer," he called out.

"Sounds good." Tessa waved back.

"Killer?" Luke asked.

Tessa giggled. "That's what Gill calls Mrs. Arbuckle's little fluff-ball of a dog. Mrs. A lives in one of our top floor suites. She's always ringing down for Gill to come walk her dog."

"Yes. I know Mrs. Arbuckle. She comes to my church. Very sweet lady." Luke smiled at Tessa, trying to ramp up the charm as much as possible. Her answering grin warmed him to the core. She was the most lovely woman he had ever seen, and exactly what he'd hoped to find in a small town like Harmony: pure, sweet and innocent.

"The coffee shop's over here." She led the way across the lobby.

# Chapter Six

Tessa's heart skipped a beat as Luke put his hand at the small of her back, guiding her through the door of the Alberta Rose Coffee Shop. His touch warmed the base of her spine, and yet sent chills right up to her head and down to her toes. He held out a chair for her, and slid it in as she sat before taking his own seat across from her. Tessa felt her face warm.

"Wow. It's been a long time since someone has shown me such chivalry," she said. Never. How about never? "Who taught you such good manners and can I send my brother there?"

Luke laughed. "Those manners were hard-learned and had to be drummed into me late in life by a local minister named Pastor Johnson. I certainly didn't learn them at home." He waved the waitress over.

Charity Wong, wearing her black hair in a short bob, walked over with a couple of menus. "Hi, Tessa. Soup of the day is cream of broccoli. What can I get you to drink?" She looked back and forth between Luke and Tessa. She met Tessa's eyes and her brows went up a fraction as if to say 'so who is this?'.

"A cola is fine," Tess answered, declining to comment on the unspoken question.

"I'll have the same," said Luke.

They chose their meals and, when Charity left with their orders, Tessa picked up the conversation. "Pastor

Johnson? Is he from around here? I don't recognize that name."

"No. I grew up in East Vancouver, just off East Hastings. It's a rough neighborhood. Thank God for the Pastor. If not for him I'd probably be either dead or in jail by now."

"Wow. That serious?" Tessa frowned. He seemed like a perfect gentleman, far from the kind of guy who'd end up in jail. Frank's brutish face came to mind and she shuddered.

"Are you cold? Would you like my jacket?"

He stood to slip off his jacket but Tessa waved him back into his chair with a smile. "I'm fine. Really." Besides, his jacket was no protection from the real threat. "Go on."

"Yeah, it was serious. I was getting more involved with one of the local gangs. It was only a matter of time before I did something really bad. That's when Pastor J stepped in."

"Your mom called him, right?" Tessa thought of her own sweet mom who would have done anything in her power to help her kids. If only she knew about Robbie, it would break her heart. Tessa was determined her mother wouldn't find out. Not if she could help it.

"My mom?" Luke laughed but it was a harsh sound so unlike his usual. Surprised, Tessa watched a shadow of anger cross his face. "No. My mom didn't care enough about me to even notice. She was too busy working the bar to care about a bastard son."

Luke stared down at his menu with great intensity for a moment, pinching the menu card so tight his fingers turned white. Finally, he took a deep breath and sighed. "Enough about me. What about you? Were you raised around here?"

Tessa smiled to hide the little surge of anxiety that raced through her. Just answer the question, Tess. Be honest to a point. There's no rule that says you have to divulge *everything* on a second date.

"I grew up in Calgary. My dad took off when I was around ten so my mom raised my brother and me alone. Money was always tight but she did a great job anyway. I've been living and working here in Harmony almost two years now."

"And your brother?" Luke took a sip of his cola.

"He's going to the University of Calgary. He works part time off campus as a waiter in one of the casinos."

"Didn't you want to go to college or anything?" Luke leaned a little closer over the table.

Tessa dropped her eyes. "Like I said, money was tight. Robbie is so smart. He's the one who could really make something of himself with a chance so we all decided he should be the one to go. He's working on a degree in Engineering."

"And you?" Luke asked. He looked at her as if he could see right through her. Tessa really didn't know how to feel about that. She so desperately wanted to confide in someone. In her heart she thought Luke was that safe, strong soul who might really be able to help. But it was just too soon to dare. She liked him. A lot. What would he think? She didn't want to burden the relationship before it had a chance to start.

"I'm happy," Tessa lied. "I love living in the mountains. I get to hike and train Otis. It's really beautiful up here." Well at least that part was true.

Charity arrived with their orders and the conversation slipped into mundane things such as Tessa's work at the hotel and Luke's coaching basketball at the local high school on Wednesday evenings. His eyes danced with enthusiasm as he talked about a few of the boys he was helping out. Tessa found herself hanging on his every word like a schoolgirl. He had such a generous heart.

As lunch wound down, Luke reached across the table and took her hand. Tessa tried to hide the little thrill of pleasure that his touch caused.

"So." He paused, clearing his throat. "Next weekend is Thanksgiving. Will you be heading into Calgary to be with your family?"

He was playing with her hand, tracing the lines on her palm with his finger. Tessa could barely concentrate on his words but forced herself to pay attention.

"No," she admitted, making a face. "I have some bills to pay so I'm picking up some extra shifts." That and she couldn't face her mom and keep her activities secret. How was it that moms could see right through you?

"Are you busy Sunday morning?"

"I usually sleep in," she answered with a smile.

"How late?" he asked.

"I don't know. Depends on if there's something to do or not. At least ten. Why?"

"How would you like to come join me at Winding River Church? It doesn't start until eleven." He smiled at her, looking hopeful. "Afterward, you could have Thanksgiving dinner with me."

"Um…" Tessa hesitated. Church? She felt her heart drop. "I'm not really into organ music," she said.

"Good. Me neither. How do you like drums, guitars, and keyboards?" Luke asked.

"That sounds more like a rock band," she said cautiously.

Luke grinned at her and said, "It is. What do you say?"

"Oh. Well," she hedged. "I'd better not. I'd probably burst into flames if I went into a church."

"An angel like you? Don't be silly. It will be fun. You'll like it," he pushed.

Smiling with her jaw clenched, she inhaled deeply causing the air to hiss softly between her teeth. "Ah, no. I don't think so. That's not the place for me. I'm sorry," she added, seeing the disappointment in his eyes.

That look was almost enough to make her change her mind. Almost. She remembered church from when she was younger and knew she wouldn't be welcome there now. Church was for good people, not people who worked the night shift like she did. And if Luke went to church, he sure wouldn't understand Misty Dawn.

Disappointment hit her with an intensity that felt like a tangible thing. Why? He was perfect in every other way. Why church? She dropped her eyes to the table.

"Are you sure?" he asked, his voice very quiet.

Tessa merely nodded. She couldn't go there. She just couldn't.

"Okay then," Luke said. She could hear the forced cheerfulness. "Thank you for having lunch with me. Can I drive you home?"

"No thanks," Tessa replied. She forced a cheerful tone as well. "I want to visit one of my friends here first. I'll see you around."

"Sure," Luke said, standing. "See you."

Tessa watched him walk up to the cashier and pay the bill before heading out the door and through the lobby. She took a deep shuddering breath. Come on, girl. It was only a couple of dates. Nothing to get your hopes up over. So what if he was the nicest, kindest, most handsome guy she'd ever met? There were plenty of guys like him out there. Right?

Tessa got up and headed out through the lobby. She had no one to see, she just needed the long walk home. As she crossed the lobby she saw Angelina, one of the front desk clerks, waving frantically at her. Reluctantly, Tessa headed over to the desk.

"*Chica!*" Angelina said under her breath, her Latina accent sneaking through in her obvious excitement. "Who was that handsome guy you were having lunch with? He is so gorgeous. *Dios Mio!*"

"That was Luke. Yeah, he is pretty hot isn't he?" Tessa's response came out flat and lifeless.

"Why the sad face?" Angelina asked. "If I'd jus' had lunch with a hunk like that I'd be floating on air." She ended her statement with a dreamy sigh and fanned herself with her hand.

"It's not going to work out, Ange." Tessa sighed. Life never worked out in her favor did it?

"What?" Angelina sounded shocked. "Why? Doesn't he like you? You are a very beautiful girl. Is he crazy?"

"No. Not that," Tessa replied. "He seems interested enough. It's just that he wants me to go to church with him."

"So?" Angelina prompted.

"So I'm not really the churchy type. I don't think I'd fit in, you know."

"Don't be silly, *Chica*," Angelina said. "Church is good for your soul. I go to mass every Sunday."

"You do?" Tessa's eyes widened. Angelina was so much fun to be around. Who'd have guessed?

"Sure. I'm a good Catholic girl." She winked and Tessa couldn't help but smile back. "Seriously though. Do you like him?"

"Yeah. I really do. He's funny and sweet, and such a gentleman," Tessa trailed off forlornly.

"Jus' go to church. You might like it. You got nothing to lose but that sexy hunk of gorgeousness."

Tessa laughed in spite of herself. "I'll think about it. What about you? Anything new in your life lately?"

"Well…" Angelina hedged. "Chef Guy *might* have cornered me in the kitchen at last night's soiree, and I *might* have let him kiss me jus' a little."

"No!" Tess breathed. "You didn't! You know he's not serious? He chases every skirt that walks by."

"That's jus' because he hasn't found the right woman yet," Angelina said with a pout.

"And you think you're the right woman to tame him? Girl. Give your head a shake!" Tessa laughed.

"You jus' wait and see, Tessa. I'll have him eating from my hand."

# Chapter Seven

A soft knock at his door interrupted Luke's reading. If you could call staring at his book but daydreaming about Tessa Peters reading. He missed her. She'd gotten completely under his skin to the point he could hardly think of anything else. He closed the book with a snap. "Come in."

Delores poked her head through the door. "Miss Riley Hamilton to see you. She's a bit early for her appointment."

"That's fine. I wasn't accomplishing much anyway. Send her right in." Luke stood up as the willowy young blonde woman came through his door.

She'd dressed casually in jeans and a pink blouse, but her belt spelled "Guess" in rhinestones, the blouse was silk, and she carried a "Coach" bag. The former thief in him quickly took note of what could fetch a good price at the pawn shop.

Her hair hung in loose waves to her shoulders. Her fine features were poised, but her eyes seemed a bit puffy and red-rimmed in spite of the careful make-up. She'd probably been crying. Luke took note of it all within seconds. He'd gotten really good at reading people during his teens living on the street.

"What can I do for you, Miss Hamilton?" Luke indicated, with a sweep of his hand, that she should take a seat in one of his easy chairs.

"Thank you," she said, perching delicately on the edge of her chair. "Please, call me Riley."

"Riley, then. How can I help you?"

"Pastor Dixon," Riley started, then cleared her throat. "As you probably know, I'm supposed to be married right here in our lovely little church in December."

"Yes, I'm aware."

"Well… It's my fiancé, Brock. He's…being difficult."

"Your fiancé is?" Luke prodded. He'd heard a few rumors of course, but not that Brock was the difficult one.

"Yes. He doesn't get along with my mother." She sighed loudly. "The truth is most people don't get along with my mother, except of course Daddy and I. And she's sweet as pie as long as you do things properly, which is to say exactly like she wants them to be done.

"But Brock needs to figure out how to humor her. She's my mom. I can't just push her out of my life like he wants me to!" Riley ended, her voice rising.

"Has he actually asked you to sever ties with her?" Luke asked.

"Well. Not in those exact words." Riley sniffed delicately.

"It's just that Mother is heavily invested in my wedding. She wants it to be perfect, you know? And Brock keeps fighting her over everything.

"I mean, yeah, she can be a little overbearing at times, but it's just because she wants the best for me. But now Brock is forcing me to choose sides. He says that if I don't side with him then he's calling off the wedding!" Riley's voice climbed into the squeaky range.

Luke watched the tears brim in her eyes as she fanned her face rapidly with one hand, trying not to cry. He pushed the box of tissues on his desk toward her. She plucked one out and dabbed at the corners of her eyes.

"He's being unreasonable. She's my mother." Riley finished with a sniff.

"What about you?" Luke asked gently.

"What do you mean?" Riley's frown barely creased her forehead.

"Forget your mother for a moment. What do *you* want for your wedding?" Luke leaned back in his chair.

Riley stared at her hands while worrying the tissue she still held. "I want Brock," she said in a small voice. "And I want a dress that suits me, not my mother's extravagant sense of style. But I can't hurt my mother. It's not fair of him to demand that.

"Can you tell him that for me? Tell Brock it's not fair to make me choose. Children are supposed to honor their mothers and fathers, aren't they? That's in the Bible somewhere, isn't it?"

"Yes. Something like that," Luke allowed. "But let's not start plucking single verses out of context to try to support our own agendas."

"But you have to help me, Pastor!" Riley's face crumpled. "I love Brock, but my mother… I can't say no to her. I don't know what to do."

"I'll do what I can to help sort this out," Luke said gently. "But first I need you to do two things for me."

Riley dabbed her eyes again and sniffed. "What do you need?"

"First, have Brock give me a call. We can meet anywhere he feels comfortable but it should be somewhere we can talk freely."

Riley nodded. "Okay. What else?"

"Second, I want you to figure out what's really important to *you*, not just for the wedding, but for the whole marriage. Write it all down. Can you do that?" Luke asked.

"Yes. Of course," Riley said, finally smiling.

The smile lit up her face and brought a sparkle back to her eyes. Luke could see what Brock found so attractive about her. Of course, she wasn't quite as stunning as Tessa was, but she was definitely a lovely girl.

"Great. I'll call you after I meet with Brock," Luke said, standing up as she rose to her feet. He walked her to the office door and watched until she drove out the church parking lot.

Luke sat heavily in his chair and ran a hand through his hair. Better call Pastor Carmichael for advice. It was a good thing the gentleman had left a number to contact him with. Luke was barely older than Riley, and not being married himself, he needed a little advice from an old pro.

# Chapter Eight

*"All employees report to the lobby immediately. All employees to the lobby, please."*

Tessa was startled to hear Manager Ben Thurston's voice on the PA system. He sounded concerned. She turned off her vacuum and dragged it out of the room she was cleaning, latching the door behind her. Leaving her maid's cart at the side of the hall, she hurried downstairs to the main lobby.

Ben stood by the front desk surrounded by most of the on-duty staff when Tessa came in. Beside him stood a young couple. Tears stained the woman's cheeks, marring her make-up. The tall man's arm wrapped protectively around her slim shoulders. Ben held up a photo of a young boy with dark hair.

"Everyone, this is Andrew. He and his parents are guests with us." Ben paused and met the woman's eyes. "Andrew has gone missing."

A general murmur rose from the group as everyone began commenting to their neighbors.

"Quiet, please." Ben waited for the shuffling and buzz of conversation to subside. "I need all staff to do a thorough search of the hotel and grounds. Andrew was last seen playing in the yard beside the outdoor patio."

"Wendy, Bailey, please check all of the offices."

Ben's sister and the hotel's accountant, Bailey, said, "On it." She was quickly followed by his eldest sister and Events Manager, Wendy.

Ben turned to his wife and PR expert, Melanie. " Mel, I need you minding the phones and coordinating our staff."

"Roberta, Angelina, leave the front desk to Melanie for now and go to all our shops and cafes. Have the staff there search their own areas."

"Chef Guy. Have your staff search the restaurant, kitchens and prep areas, especially the walk-in freezer."

"*Mais oui!* Right away. To the kitchen!" he commanded. The charming French master chef marshaled his staff and hurried off toward the kitchens.

"Gill, take some of the porters and search the basement and parking lot."

"Vera, have the housekeeping staff search their respective floors carefully. Make sure to check in the cleaning closets. He might have got himself locked in somewhere by accident."

Vera Dietrich, head of housekeeping, clapped her hands loudly several times. She looked like a short fat commandant. "You heard him, ladies. Let's go!"

Tessa turned to go but heard Ben call out, "Tessa, not you. Come see me in a moment. Everyone else, go now and search. Inform Melanie the moment you find Andrew. Otherwise meet outside in the main parking lot as soon as your area is searched. I'll be contacting the firehall to organize the search outdoors."

Tessa approached Ben as the other staff scattered to search their areas. His hair was disheveled as if he'd run his fingers through it a couple dozen times. Ben was speaking softly with the couple who must be Andrew's parents.

"You wanted to see me, sir?" Tessa asked.

"Yes." He turned toward her at the sound of her voice. "You're training your dog to search, yes?"

"Yes, sir. I'm not sure he's ready for a real mission yet. I'm still in the process of training him."

"Go get him anyway. It can't hurt. Meet us in the parking lot as soon as possible."

"Yes, sir. I'll need a scent article sir."

"A what?" Ben asked, sounding stressed.

"Something that smells like Andrew, like a shirt."

"Robert," Andrew's mom said. "His pajama top. It's upstairs in the room."

"I'll get it, Evelyn," Robert said, and rushed toward the elevators.

Fifteen minutes later, Tessa was pulling her little car back into the hotel parking lot amid a gathering crowd of staff and townsfolk. She noticed Luke's red truck and her heart gave a little leap in her chest. She squashed it back down. That relationship was not going to work. She needed to get that firmly in her mind and limit her exposure to Luke until she stopped feeling giddy every time she looked at him.

She clipped Otis' leash on him before getting out of the car, and kept a firm grip on him amid the crowd. She caught a glimpse of Logan Wright, one of Harmony's firemen, coordinating the search. Tall and muscular, with his receding hair shaved short, he was standing in front of the fire truck and speaking with Ben. Tessa hurried over to where they stood.

"I'm here," she announced.

"Good," Logan said brusquely. "I want you to go to the yard by the patio and see if your dog can pick up Andrew's scent."

"Here." Ben offered over a blue pajama top. "Andrew's dad brought this down."

45

"Thanks," Tessa said, taking the top from Ben. "I'll get going right away."

"No," Logan said firmly. "No one goes out alone."

"I have Otis. I don't need anyone else," Tessa insisted.

"You need a partner. Where's that new guy? He isn't paired up yet." Logan peered out through the remainder of the quickly dispersing crowd.

New guy? Tessa's pulse jumped. There was only one new guy in town that she knew of, and she didn't want to be out alone with him. It was hard enough longing for what might have been without having to look at him all day.

"There he is. Hey! You!" Logan called out, waving.

Tessa followed his line of sight to Luke, looking handsome as ever in his fitted jeans and navy sweater. He saw her looking at him, and their eyes met as he headed her way. Tessa glanced down at herself. She still wore the muted emerald green scrub uniform that was the garb of all the cleaning staff at the hotel. Great. There was a stain on her pants, and she was sure she smelled like bathroom disinfectant. Oh well. Seeing her look like this should chase him away for good.

Otis yanked his leash, leaping forward with his tail fanning when Luke walked up. He jumped up and Luke caught his front paws, dropping them down and bending to scratch his chest. "Hello, boy. How's a good fellow?"

"Good," Logan said. "I see you don't mind dogs. I'm going to pair you up with Tessa and her dog. See if Otis can pick up Andrew's trail. Here's a radio. Call in if you find anything at all. I'll be here co-ordinating until we find him. I'll radio you when it's time to come back."

Luke took the radio from Logan. "Got it." He turned to Tessa. "Ready?"

"I guess so." What was she supposed to say? No. I can't go paired with you? She'd have to explain why. She couldn't tell him he was charming and sexy and she could barely think straight with him standing beside her. "Otis, heel," she said instead, and headed toward the rear of the hotel where the patio backed onto a green space and Harmony Creek.

Luke walked beside her in silence. She glanced briefly his way only to find his eyes locked on her. She looked away quickly. Tessa had no mystical Jedi training. She couldn't control "the force". So why could she feel Luke watching her? It was unnerving, or perhaps exciting.

"Why are you staring at me?" she asked, stopping abruptly to face him.

"Was I staring? Sorry. It's just that you look beautiful today," he replied.

"Oh." What does one say to that? She looked down at herself. "I'm just in my uniform. It's not even clean."

"It brings out the green in your eyes. And the messy bun suits you." He smiled then, and Tessa's heart melted. She could feel the heat creep into her cheeks.

"Um. Thanks." She tucked a stray lock of hair back into place. She always wore her hair in a bun while working as a maid. For one thing it kept it out of her face while bending over to clean under things. For another, it made her look vastly different from Misty Dawn. She didn't want any of the hotel guests who might catch her late night show to recognize her at her day job. She wanted to keep those jobs, those lives, completely separate. Tessa wasn't that kind of girl, and Misty Dawn? Misty did what needed to be done.

"Here we are." Tessa led the way as they approached the outdoor patio and manicured lawn surrounding the hotel.

The Thurston Hotel sat prominently on Main Street in the heart of downtown Harmony. Behind it, to the south, Harmony Creek flowed fresh and clear down from the Rocky Mountains in the west, through a green space that separated the town from the golf course. Hotel guests loved having the golf course just a five minute walk across the footpath bridge, but now it meant there were acres of land in which a small boy could get lost. Fortunately, being autumn, the creek was low and not a great drowning threat. Still, if he had slipped and hit his head, he could drown in only a couple of inches of water.

"Otis," Tessa said, pulling out the pajama top. She held it out for the dog to smell. "Suche, Otis." The Shepherd snuffed at the shirt, then Tessa directed his attention to the ground.

"Suche!" she commanded.

Otis began casting back and forth with his nose hovering just off the ground. It took a few minutes of weaving before he changed directions and began heading across the lawn to where the native Balsam Poplar, White Birch, and Alpine Larch intermingled on the creek bank. Tessa let out the twenty foot lead she was holding and followed behind the dog.

"Do you think he has the scent?" Luke asked. "It's already four o'clock. The sun will be setting in a couple of hours and then it will get cold quickly."

"I know. It's already chilly. That breeze off the mountains smells like winter. We can only hope Otis has the right scent. He's still not finished training so I'm not sure."

Otis followed along a faint path heading upstream toward Harmony's off-lead dog park. The park was located on a small island in the middle of the creek and accessible by a little foot bridge. Just before the bridge, Otis stopped suddenly and pressed his nose to the ground. He made a loud sniffing noise, then veered off sharply and began moving further upstream, past the small island.

"He's definitely got something now," Tessa said breathlessly, hurrying to keep up with Otis as he pulled her onward.

Otis led them across rough grass and through low scrubby bush, in an erratic pattern. They came close to the creek a few times but stayed on the north bank. The sweet scent of poplar and tang of pine spiced the fall air.

"Are you sure he's on the right scent?" Luke asked. "He's dragging us all over the place."

"I don't know," Tessa replied breathlessly. "I hope so."

Otis had picked up speed and was dragging Tessa at a brisk walk through dry forest along the creek. He stopped suddenly to stuff his head into a low dense bush, tail held in a high arc. Tessa took two steps closer when a large snowshoe hare exploded out from the bush. With ears and legs already turning white for the winter, it was easy to spot, and Otis leapt after it instantly. Eighty pounds of solid muscle hurtling at top speed snapped the leash taut and yanked Tessa off her feet. She flew forward, crashing into the underbrush and sliding a few feet before the leash slipped off her wrist.

"Tessa!" Luke called out, as he ran to where she'd fallen.

"Ow," she moaned under her breath. "Stupid dog." She rolled gingerly onto her back with the dry leaves and twigs crackling under her.

"Are you all right?" Luke crouched down at her side. Worry creased his face and Tessa felt a surge of pleasure to think he cared. "Don't move."

"I'll be fine." She tried to ignore the ache in her shoulder. "Help me up."

"Wait. You're bleeding."

Tessa struggled to prop herself onto her elbows and looked down toward her legs. There was a long tear in her scrub pants at the left groin and a growing blood stain. "Oooo…" She let herself flop onto her back again and closed her eyes tightly.

"Are you all right? Tessa?" Luke bent closer to her, placing his hand along her cheek. It felt warm and comforting there, but Tessa resisted the urge to turn in closer.

"I'll be okay," she said in a faint voice. "Blood makes me kind of squeamish."

He chuckled softly. "And you want to do search and rescue?"

"Well, it's mostly my own blood that makes me squeamish, not other people's."

Luke laughed outright at that. "Here, I brought some first aid supplies in my backpack."

He slipped a small bag off his shoulders and rummaged inside for a moment before bringing out a box of gauze squares.

"We'll just have to…ah…um…" He paused, gauze in hand, as a faint flush reddened his cheeks.

Tessa followed his line of sight back to her wound and it didn't take long to realize why. The rip was very close to her most private place. She glanced back at him and felt a warm surge of gratitude. Most men would have been more than happy to rip her pants off.

"I'm sorry, Tessa, but we'll have to slide your pants down a bit to clean this up," Luke said. "I'd suggest you bandage yourself, but you still look a little peaked."

"No, you do it. I can't look," she said, closing her eyes and lying flat again.

Luke gently undid the string tightening her scrubs around her waist and loosened them. He took hold of each pant leg at the side of her thighs. "Now lift your hips," he said. Tessa did and Luke carefully slid the pants down just enough to expose the wound in her groin.

Belatedly, Tessa wondered if she had nice panties on or her awful granny panties. It shouldn't matter, because she had decided Luke was just not her type, but it was suddenly very important to know. She snuck a peek down and felt a surge of relief to see the gray and white leopard print with the lilac lace trim. She closed her eyes again as Luke rummaged in his pack for supplies.

"Here." Luke took her cold left hand in his big warm one. He directed it toward her panty leg hole. "Just pull up a little here, so I can get at your wound."

Tessa pulled up on the panties at the leg. A little shiver ran through her at Luke's gentle touch on her skin. He was very careful to keep his hands professional, but the odd brush of his hand on her skin drove her wild.

"This might sting a bit," he apologized in advance.

"Ow," Tessa hissed as a peroxide-soaked gauze pressed into the crease of her leg.

"Sorry. I have to get it clean. You don't want it to get infected." He wiped gently then said, "It looks like a pretty deep gouge, but I don't think it will need stitches. What's this other mark here? I don't think it's a bruise because it's brownish."

"That's just my birthmark. It's a 'Cafe-Au-Lait' spot. I've had it all my life."

"Well, the stick that stabbed you went right through it," Luke said quietly. "It kind of looks like a heart shape doesn't it?" He tipped his head to one side, viewing it intently.

Tessa peered down at her groin. "I hadn't noticed before from this angle, but looking at it from your position, yeah, I guess it does."

Seeing Luke's hand gently pressing gauze into her groin, noticing how close his hand was to her sensitive zone, sent a flood of heat pulsing through her. She imagined his hand straying, caressing her, stroking her to heights of passion. Her leg throbbed, whether from pain or excitement she wasn't sure.

Her eyes travelled from his hand, slowly up his arm, across his hard muscular chest and came to rest on his eyes. A deep gray-blue storm raged in those eyes, a hunger that seemed to match her own.

Luke cleared his throat abruptly and averted his eyes. "I should tape this up. We need to find Otis too."

Otis! How could she forget him so quickly? "Otis come!" she bellowed from her spot on the ground.

Kneeling beside her in the brush, Luke took a dry gauze square, folded it once, and taped it securely to her skin. When he was done, Tessa gently tugged her pants back up and tied her string.

"Can you stand up?" Luke offered her his hand as he stood himself.

Tessa accepted his hand, allowing herself to be pulled upright. She wobbled slightly as she stood, and Luke immediately pulled her against his chest, cradling her there. "Easy does it," he crooned. "Are you going to be okay?"

*Okay*? She'd be okay forever if she could just stay like this; sheltered in his arms, head pressed to his chest, the erratic beat of his heart in her ear. Such a warm safe place to be.

She sighed softly. "Yes. Just a little light-headed for a moment."

She tried to lean away but he resisted her attempt. She looked up, noticed the pulse throbbing by his throat, and let her eyes drift higher until they met his. He reached up and brushed a strand of hair from her face, letting his hand linger on her cheek.

"You have a smudge," he murmured, using his thumb to wipe the corner of her mouth.

Tessa's pulse raced, and warmth surged through her. Her lips parted in invitation. He moved in closer, his blue eyes searching her face. His face dipped closer and Tessa dropped her eyelids.

His lips met hers, soft yet persuasive. Tessa melted into him, using his strong body to keep herself from falling. Pulsing heat surged through her as his kiss deepened, silently asking more of her. Her fingers clutched onto his sweater, kneading the muscles beneath. He shivered beneath her fingertips and moved his hand up, cupping the back of her head, while never ceasing the assault of his lips on hers.

With a crash, Otis blasted back through the underbrush and jumped up at Tessa, tongue lolling halfway to the ground. Luke took a couple of steps back, still breathing hard. Tessa felt the separation like a cold wind, immediately missing his touch.

"Sorry," he said gruffly. "I shouldn't have taken advantage of you like that." He turned away from her and gathered up the first aid supplies from his backpack.

He was sorry? The disappointment hit her hard. She wasn't sorry. She had wanted more. Much more. She turned her attention back to Otis.

"Come here, bad dog," she said gently.

She had just untangled Otis' leash when the radio squawked, "Andrew has been found. Repeat. Andrew has been found. All volunteers back to the hotel."

"Time to go back," Luke said brusquely, still avoiding eye contact.

"I'm so glad they found him," Tessa said. "Otis, heel!"

It only took a few steps for Tessa to realize that, while nothing was broken, she was wrenched and bruised and limping nonetheless. After a few painful yards, Luke stopped her.

"Here, give me the leash," he said.

"I can manage," Tessa protested.

"Just give it," Luke persisted. He took the lead from her, then bent and scooped her off her feet into his arms.

"Whoa! What are you doing?" she asked, trying not to enjoy herself too much and just a little afraid of how much she did.

"I'll carry you back. You're still sore. I can tell."

"You can't carry me all that way," she said. "I'm too heavy."

"Nah. It's not that far and you're not heavy. What are you? 115? 120 pounds?"

"I'm 130 pounds," Tessa corrected.

"See? Light as a feather."

He walked her along the creek as if she weighed nothing, and Tessa soon found herself relaxing into his secure hold. Her head tipped to rest on his shoulder. She could see the hint of golden stubble across his jaw and smell the spicy scent of his aftershave mingled with hot man. A little voice in her head whispered that she hadn't felt this safe in a long time, not since her dad had abandoned them. It was a nice feeling and she soaked it up, fearing it couldn't last for long.

People were still milling about in the parking lot when they got back. Luke carried her all the way to her car before lowering her feet to the ground. She tried to slip from his arms but he tightened his hold. She looked up to meet his stormy blue gaze.

"I don't want to let you go," he said softly.

"Yeah?" Tessa felt her face flush. *I don't want you to let me go either.* "We can't just stand here all night. People will stare."

"Let them stare. I missed you this week," Luke said. "I can't seem to get you out of my head." His hand ran up and down her spine in a gentle caress.

"Me too," she acknowledged softly, leaning into his warmth.

"So it wasn't too awful, being paired up with me today? I saw the look on your face when Logan suggested it."

She smiled into his sweater and hugged him. "Not too awful."

A soft chuckle rumbled in his chest, then he took a deep breath, holding it a moment before finally saying, "Meet me at church Sunday? Please? Just give it a try?"

Tessa stilled in his arms as she considered the idea. She used to love going to church with her mom. Was it worth a try? What if they found out about her other job? They would hate her, wouldn't they? But how would they find out? Surely none of those people went to The Wobbly Dog.

And what about Luke? Being here in his arms felt so wonderful. He was so different from most of the men she had known. Was church the reason? Angelina thought she should try it.

If she went, and it was awful, that would settle it for her, but why drag this out? She should just end this charade once and for all and stop tormenting herself.

*No thanks.* But the words wouldn't come out of her mouth. She didn't want this embrace to end, couldn't bear the thought of walking away for good. She wasn't good for him, she knew that, but he seemed to be good for her.

"What time?" she asked. No, no, no! Silly girl, say you can't make it.

"It starts at eleven but be there a bit before. I get there early so I'll save you a seat," he said, grinning ear to ear. "Are you okay to drive home?"

"I'll be fine." Tessa found herself smiling in spite of her misgivings.

Luke tipped her chin up toward him and planted a swift tender kiss on her lips. "I'll take the radio back. See you Sunday."

He finally released her and Tessa stepped back, instantly missing his embrace. She watched him cross the parking lot toward the fire truck with a multitude of conflicting emotions warring within her. She lifted a hand to touch her lip where it tingled from his kiss, and found that she was smiling in spite of all her misgivings. Only two more days until she could see him again.

Only two more nights dancing.

Her stomach clenched.

# Chapter Nine

Tessa sat in her car. The bright red roof on the white church building gave it a cheery look, but her stomach danced with butterflies regardless. She stared at the people going up the wide front steps and through the double main doors. Some people were dressed up, but others just wore jeans. Tessa looked down at her modest navy shirt-dress. At least clothing-wise, it seemed she'd fit in. Everyone had disappeared inside, but still she remained there. She glanced at her watch: 10:58. She took a deep breath.

"Okay. Now or never." Tessa emerged from her car.

Her heart fluttered in her chest as she climbed the three steps to the landing in front of the doors. She took another deep breath, pulled open the door, and stepped through. A spacious lobby with medium blue carpet lay before her. To her right was a door labelled nursery. To her left were the washrooms and a hallway to the office. Straight before her, across the lobby, were two wide mahogany doors leading to the sanctuary beyond.

Many people were still milling about in the lobby as Tessa stepped in. She clutched her handbag in front of her as if it were a shield. A plump older woman with short gray hair and a smiling, unlined face approached with her hand outstretched in greeting. Her grasp was warm and firm as she shook Tessa's hand.

"Hello. I'm Delores. Are you Tessa by any chance?"

"Um. Yes. I am," Tessa admitted.

"Oh good. Pastor Dixon will be so pleased," Delores said, smiling warmly.

Pastor Dixon? Why would the pastor be pleased? Maybe Luke had told him she was coming.

"Luke!" Delores called out, waving.

Across the lobby, the two doors to the sanctuary stood propped open. Rows of neat gray upholstered chairs were arranged on either side of a center aisle. Pot lights covered the ceiling in the well-lit room, creating an inviting atmosphere. Up front, two steps led to a wide stage where several musicians were tuning an assortment of instruments.

Luke was standing part way down the aisle talking to a young couple, but turned toward them at Delores' call.

Tessa watched as Luke caught sight of her. His grin was instantaneous and blinding. She couldn't help but grin back at his enthusiasm. Luke immediately excused himself and headed their way.

He wore jeans and a black T-shirt with a gray blazer over top. Somehow he managed to look casual and dressed up at the same time.

"Tessa. I'm so glad you came," Luke said. "I see you've met Delores. She's secretary here at the church. Thank you, Delores. I've got this."

Delores smiled and patted his arm. "I'm sure you do."

Turning to Tessa she said, "I hope you can join us for Thanksgiving dinner after church. I've invited Luke to join my granddaughter and me for dinner. We'd love for you to come too."

"Well…If you're sure that you don't mind," Tessa replied.

"Of course not, dear. You're more than welcome." Delores' warm smile put Tessa at ease.

"Thank you. I'd love to."

Luke took her hand in his. "Your fingers are freezing," he commented. He raised her hand and kissed the back of her fingers. It was only a brief moment, but the rush of heat spread through her until her cheeks glowed.

"Let's go sit. I've saved us a seat at the front," Luke said.

He started leading her down the aisle. The front?

"There are lots of seats back here," she said, indicating the back row with her hand and lagging behind, trying to slow his forward momentum.

"I always sit at the front," he answered, not slowing his pace.

"But..," Tessa's protest faded out as he almost dragged her to the front row and sat her beside him next to the aisle.

On the low stage before them, a guitarist, bass player, keyboardist, drummer and a couple of people with microphones milled about, getting organized. A moment later, the first chord rang out. Everyone got to their feet and began to sing and clap along to the music.

Tessa stood too, just trying to fit in. Beside her, Luke's strong tenor rang out. She glanced over. He seemed so happy to be here. She peeked at a few other faces. They all seemed happy. This was far from the solemn services she remembered as a kid. Tessa found herself singing along, following the words that were projected on the drop-down screen at the front.

When the singing stopped, Delores stepped up to the stage and made a few announcements. The drive for the food bank had been a big success. The youth were to meet for basketball Wednesday night at the middle school gym down the block as usual. There was a harvest party planned for Saturday the twenty-ninth for the youth and adult volunteers were needed to help out.

"Now, let's have a warm welcome as Pastor Dixon brings us today's message," Delores concluded.

Beside her, Luke stood to his feet and moved toward the stage. Tessa tried to peer past him, down the row, to see who Pastor Dixon might be, but no one else seemed to be moving. Confused, she looked back at Luke who had moved to the podium and was putting down some papers and a Bible.

"Good morning, Church," he said. "Isn't it great day to be here?"

Tessa's mouth dropped open. What was going on? Why was Luke up there? Where was Pastor Dixon? She looked back over her shoulder at all the faces eagerly listening to Luke. She turned back toward him, still stunned. He caught her glance and winked at her, never missing a beat in his message. She returned his smile in a tight, strained sort of way.

*Luke* was the pastor? It sank in slowly. When he'd said it was 'his church' she'd thought he just meant the church he went to. She'd never dreamed he meant he was *pastor*. She swallowed hard.

Now what? What was she even doing here? She really didn't fit in, or at least Misty didn't. On the other hand, no one knew her alter ego. No one would suspect. Besides, she couldn't very well get up in the middle and run out. That would be embarrassing. Best to just sit here and pretend to belong.

Having decided to just go with the flow, Tessa focused her attention back onto Luke's message. He was talking about mistakes, and forgiveness, and trusting God with your problems. Most of it applied to her life. In fact, some of it was so darn close she began to wonder if Luke knew more about her weekend activities than he let on.

As she listened, memories of Sundays with her mom flooded back. Sitting on the hard pews, nestled into the

crook of her mother's arm, all had seemed well. Even
after her dad had left, they still went. Her mom had
seemed to draw comfort from being there, and as long as
Mom was happy, Tessa had been happy too. When she hit
her teens, she'd drifted from church, caught up in more
important things. Church was dull. Who needed it?

Then Robbie had screwed up big time. He had
confided in Tessa first, and neither of them had the heart
to tell their mom what he'd done. Mom had worked so
hard to look after them, it would break her heart to find
out the truth.

Tessa couldn't abandon Robbie to his fate, so she had
stepped in to solve the problem the only way she could
think of. After that she had longed for the comfort of
church, but she just couldn't bring herself to sit there
Sunday morning knowing what she was doing on Friday
and Saturday nights. So she had stayed away. Until now.

Luke's message was hitting home. A deep longing
welled up within her. Maybe if she came back to church,
God would help her out of the mess she was in. Maybe
there was hope after all.

Luke closed with prayer, then the band started up one
more time, and he came back off the stage to stand
beside her. He smiled down at her, and laced his fingers
between hers, then turned his attention back to the front
and sang along with the music.

Tessa stared at their hands, hers looking so small and
pale nestled into his large tanned one. His message had
been so close to the truth. Did he know?

The music faded out, and everyone began to gather
their things.

"I have to go shake a few hands. Meet me in the
lobby in ten minutes?"

"Sure," she said. She made her way slowly toward the lobby while thoughts warred in her head. How much did he know?

She positioned herself discreetly by the coat rack where she could watch Luke interact with the people. He greeted everyone, smiling, shaking hands, and often bestowing hugs as they left. Delores gave him a big hug on her way out. He seemed well loved.

Tessa felt an ache in her chest. She used to belong, too. Now she didn't even feel at home at her mom's house with the secret she kept. She couldn't tell her mom, she just couldn't, and she couldn't look her in the eye and not confess everything either. So she stayed away.

She watched as Luke bade farewell to the last person and turned back to where she waited.

"Sorry that took so long. People love to chat Sunday morning." He walked over and took her coat off the rack, holding it open so she could slip her arms in. "It's still pretty warm for October. Want to just walk to Delores' house? It's only a couple of blocks over."

"Sure." She wrapped a long lacy wool scarf around her neck and stood rigid, her fingers fidgeting with the fringed ends. What did he know? What should she tell him? What should she do?

Tessa clutched her coat around her as they left the church. The sun was bright and warm where it reached, but the wind had a chill edge to it as the coming winter whispered off the mountains. Her mind raced in circles as they strolled down the sidewalk.

"You're awfully quiet today. Is everything okay?" Luke squeezed her hand gently.

Tessa hesitated. What should she say? Finally she said, "You didn't tell me you were the pastor."

"I didn't?" He sounded surprised. "I'm sorry. I thought you knew. I thought everyone in this little town knew. Does that...change things? Between us I mean."

Did it? Maybe. Maybe not. She couldn't imagine a pastor would want to date a stripper. But then Luke probably wouldn't want to date one even if he wasn't a pastor. So nothing had changed, really.

Tessa cleared her throat. "Have you been...watching me?"

"Watching you? I can't take my eyes off you when you're around if that's what you mean." He smiled but she could see the worry in his eyes.

"No. I mean, have you been... following me or..." She looked down at the toes of her boots.

"You mean stalking you?" Luke sounded incredulous. "No. Of course not. Why would you even think that?"

"It's that sermon you just preached. It's like you were reading my thoughts or... or watching me, or..."

"Oh," Luke said, as if every crazy word she'd just spoken made perfect sense. "Is that all?"

She scowled at him. "What's that supposed to mean?"

He reached out and took her hand in his as they walked. "I wrote that sermon about four weeks ago, before I met you. It's part of a series I planned out to end on Thanksgiving."

"How is that possible? It seemed like you aimed it right at me," Tessa said.

Luke chuckled. "Yes. I've felt the same way when Pastor Johnson used to preach. Sometimes, when the sermon seems as if it's made just for you, that's because God is trying to talk to you. Now all you have to do, is decide if you want to listen or not.

"Is this all brand new to you? Have you never been to church before?" Luke asked.

What to say? She gazed up at the mountains, gathering her thoughts. "I used to go all the time with my mom, but when I hit high school there were sports, and friends, and I guess I just lost interest. Then some things… happened. I wasn't sure I could come back."

"You can always come back," Luke said gently. He stopped and indicated the neat little two story home in front of them. "This is Delores' house."

"Oh. I guess we should go in," Tessa said.

"Or, we can walk around the block again if you'd like."

Tessa stood in front of him for a moment. She ran her fingers up and down the lapel of his gray wool coat, then stopped. "Will God really forgive anything?"

"Anything," Luke assured her. "If you need proof just look at me."

She smiled at that. "Then I think that I want to come back. If you're sure God wants me." She looked up into his eyes, feeling hopeful for the first time in nearly two years.

Luke's answering smile was blinding. "I'm sure. So. Is there anything you want to confess?"

"I thought pastors didn't do confession." She gave him a sideways look.

"They don't." He laughed. "I'm just giving you the opportunity to get things off your chest."

"Then I confess that I'm starving and Mrs. Reid's turkey smells heavenly." She didn't need to tell him now. She could tell him later. Maybe a lot later. Or maybe she could just fix this whole mess and never have to tell him at all. That sounded like the best plan of them all.

"Let's go." Luke took her hand again and headed up to the door.

# Chapter Ten

"He's doing much better, don't you think?" Luke asked Tessa as they walked back to his truck after a couple hours of training with Otis. They had gone out Thanksgiving Monday, Thursday after work, and again this afternoon.

"Yes. Definitely." Tessa reached out to stroke Otis' head. "You're a good boy, aren't you? Yes, you are."

"Why do people always use those goofy voices when they talk to their pets?" Luke asked, chuckling at her.

"Who you calling goofy?" She threw a mock punch toward his shoulder.

His hand shot out, caught her wrist and quickly tugged her toward him. He caught her about the waist with his other arm, trapping her. "Gotcha!"

Tessa laughed. Pressed against him, her soft curves molding against the hard muscle of his thighs and chest, she felt her face heat up and her heart throb.

"Wow. That was fast," she said breathlessly."

"Uh huh," he acknowledged. "You can take a punk off the street, but you can't take the street out of the man he becomes. I still have great reflexes."

"I can see that," she murmured, leaning in. She looked up into his eyes, as dark and wild as a stormy sea, watched his gaze as they moved over her face, seeming to notice every detail. She saw him pause on her mouth, linger there. She held her breath, waiting for his kiss, longing for it.

"I feel like the luckiest man in the world," he said, his voice soft and husky. He reached up and tucked a strand of hair that had escaped her ponytail back behind her ear. "Here I am, in this beautiful place, with the most beautiful girl in the world in my arms." He let his hand slide back to her waist.

Tessa flushed with pleasure. From where their bodies touched, she could feel his desire. It fired her own passion. Her breasts tingled where they pressed into his chest. The hand at the small of her back did a slow gentle knead. Her body flushed with heat, as if fire raced through her veins like nothing she'd ever felt before.

She leaned in. *Kiss me!*

He suddenly released her, bringing her trapped hand up to his mouth and kissing her knuckles instead. He cleared his throat and stepped back, running one hand through his hair.

Tessa deflated like a popped balloon. Why'd he put on the brakes? Was he not feeling the same rush of desire she was?

He turned away from her, flinging his arms wide, indicating everything around them. "I mean look at this place. Isn't it gorgeous?"

"Yes. It's amazing," Tessa answered flatly. Why would he back away from her? Could he sense she was keeping something from him?

Tessa bit her lip. Maybe she should confide in him. Maybe he could help somehow. But what could he possibly do? He wasn't much older than her twenty-four years, and she doubted pastors made tons of money.

What if he didn't like what he heard? She pictured his warm generous mouth curling in disgust. His eyes so filled with kindness turning hard and cold. She couldn't bear the thought. She wanted his smile, his kiss, his embrace.

Oh God! She loved him. Her eyes widened as the realization hit. She loved him!

"What's the matter?" Luke asked. "You look like you've seen a ghost."

"Me? Nah. I'm fine." She flashed her biggest fake please-the-Friday-night-drunks smile to bolster her words. "Let's load Otis in the truck and head back to town."

Otis leapt into the back seat of Luke's small quad cab while Tessa climbed in the front. Her mind was still racing when Luke hopped into the driver's seat.

"Can we stop at Pet World before you take me home?" she asked. "I'm almost out of dog food, and it's cheaper to buy the giant bags, but those are difficult for me to carry."

"No problem," Luke answered. "Your wish is my command."

""Thanks," she said, still pensive.

"You sure you're okay?" he asked. "You're not worried about something?"

"Of course not. So... You've never told me about your parents." That's right, Tess. Change the subject fast.

"I guess I haven't. There's not much to tell. My mom worked a lot. On the night shift. She slept late every day. We had a falling out when I hit my teens," Luke said. "I never knew my father. He took off when I was just a baby, so I never had a dad of any sort."

"Your mom never remarried?" Tessa asked.

"I don't think she ever got married in the first place," Luke said, scowling at the gravel road ahead. "And none of the losers she brought home could qualify as dad material. No. The closest thing I ever had to a dad was Pastor Johnson. He's the greatest man I ever knew."

"He sure made an impression on you," Tessa said.

"He did more than make an impression. He probably saved my life."

"That's a bit dramatic," Tessa commented. "Did he really?"

"You tell me," Luke replied. "I was a fifteen-year-old kid, running with a gang, on the verge of dropping out of school, selling drugs and getting high. How many people like that in the downtown east side live to a ripe old age?"

"Not many, I guess," Tessa answered. Vancouver's downtown east side was notorious for drugs, prostitution, and crime. It wouldn't have been an easy place to grow up in.

"Not unless they leave the lifestyle. Pastor Johnson was my way out. He looked past the punk I was to the person God intended me to be. He showed me love, and a better way to live. Until him, I thought I was on my own. He taught me there is always help for those who ask," Luke said.

"He sounds like a nice man. I hope I can meet him one day," Tessa said wistfully.

"I hope you will too." Luke turned off Cougar Road and into town, moving slowly on the crowded little streets..

His words rattled around in her head. *There's always help for those who ask.* Maybe she should ask for help. It had worked for him. It might work for her too.

"Here we are. Pet World." Luke drove slowly down Elk Street. "But all the curbside spots are full. I didn't realize Saturday afternoons were so busy."

"Just park in the bus depot lot," Tessa advised. "That's where I usually park. It's only half a block away. We can walk if you don't mind carrying the dog food for me."

"Sure thing," Luke said cheerfully.

He parked near the corner, and hopped out to come around and open her door. She zipped her jacket up a little higher before climbing out. They left the window down a bit for Otis who sat with his nose pressed against the glass as they left.

They started walking east on Elk Street, past the Pancake House on the corner, then past The Wobbly Dog. Tessa watched the front door as they walked past, fearful someone would come out who'd recognize her. Why had she suggested they park at the bus depot? That was a dumb idea.

Luke completely ignored the place as they walked by. He talked to her of other things, not noticing she was distracted. She couldn't keep her mind focused. What would he think if he knew? Would he love her anyway, or would he dump her? Did he even love her to begin with?

Luke held open the door for her at Pet World, and followed her to the dog food section where he easily picked up the massive bag of food she wanted. He waited patiently for her as she paid, then hoisted the bag up onto his right shoulder to carry back through the door. He offered her his hand as they left, and Tessa took it, letting her fingers entwine between his.

They walked back toward his truck. Tessa's eyes glued themselves to The Dog again. *Tell him.* But how?

"Hey. I'm starving," she started. "Want to get a bite before I have to go home?"

"Sure." He grinned. "I always want to spend more time with you. The Pancake House sound good?"

It was on her lips to say, yes. But she needed to tell him. How could she tell him? Maybe if…

"How about here?" She indicated The Wobbly Dog with her hand, hoping he wouldn't notice it shaking. "I hear they have the best Jerk chicken wings."

"There?" Luke's lip curled. "No thanks. I don't do places like that. Ever. I don't care how good the wings are."

"Oh." Tessa felt her heart drop. At least she knew he hadn't been following or watching her.

"Besides," Luke continued, "I'd never take an angel like you into a disgusting hell-hole like that. Let's drop off the dog food in the truck then go to The Pancake House. Otis will be fine for a while, and I'd like to buy you dinner." He flashed her a huge smile.

Tessa tried to smile back but her face felt stiff. He'd called it a hell-hole. He didn't even want her to eat there. He'd freak if he found out she worked there.

"Are you sure you're okay, Tessa? Is there something on your mind? Something you want to talk about?" he asked, touching her shoulder.

"What? Me? No...Of course not." She forced herself to smile.

"Are you sure? I'm here for you, if you need something." His concern sounded genuine. If only he knew...

"I'm just tired. I worked late last night and have another late shift tonight. Maybe we should skip The Pancake House this time. I need to take a nap before I go to work."

"You work so much. Can't the hotel hire another maid so you don't have to work every weekend?" Luke asked.

"It's not the hotel's fault. I need the extra money. I'm just paying off a small loan. It should be almost paid off." Her conscience poked at her for letting him believe she was working for the hotel, but she pushed it down. He hadn't actually asked if that's where she was working. Technically, she wasn't lying to him. So why did she feel so guilty?

"How much is still outstanding, if that isn't too nosy of me," he asked.

"I...I'm not exactly sure. I haven't checked lately." And Marco doesn't give me a balance sheet.

"It should be printed on your last bill," Luke offered.

"Right. I'll...check later."

Luke loaded the bag of food into the bed of his truck then held open the door for her while she got in. They drove the short distance to her home in silence.

"I can take the bag from here." Tessa climbed out the door of his truck.

"Nonsense. I've got it," Luke countered. "Just grab Otis. I'll get the kibble." He went to the back and scooped up the heavy bag, carrying it easily to her door.

"Just put it there in the entranceway," she said, taking Otis to the back yard and turning him loose there.

She returned to her door to find Luke standing there, fidgeting while he waited. She gazed up at him while his eyes roved over her face.

"Let me try something," he murmured.

She waited while his hands reached past her face and slipped the pony elastic from her hair. It fell in loose silken waves around her face. He fluffed it out with his fingertips, a slow smile spreading across his face.

"There. Like dark honey and gold," he said, his eyes flicking back and forth, looking her over. "You should wear it like this more often. You're absolutely gorgeous." He left his hands resting gently on her shoulders...

Tessa felt her face warm, and a slow heat crept through her body at his compliment. "Thank you," she murmured.

He paused, watching her, then slowly tipped her chin up and moved in until his lips met hers in a deep probing kiss that left her pulse bouncing and her breath ragged.

She reached up, skimming her hands across his chest and looping them behind his neck. She pulled him closer, pressing her breasts against his chest and feeling his body respond to hers. He wrapped his arms around her, pulling her tighter, while his mouth explored hers. Need swelled within her, a dull pulse between her thighs.

"Come inside with me," she whispered, breaking their kiss.

She looked up. His eyes had darkened to a deep blue-gray. His chest heaved as he took a step back, breaking contact with her.

"I...I should go. You need to sleep and I... need to control myself better."

"Do you have to?" she asked. *Don't go. I need you.* She swallowed a lump in her throat.

"I have to...Will I see you? Tomorrow, at church?"

"Yes. Of course," she replied. *Anywhere. I'll follow you anywhere.*

"Good." He took a couple of steps backward, and with a last look, turned away and walked back to his truck.

Tessa watched him go, her body still humming from his touch. Her heart ached with its newfound revelation. How could the town's most reluctant stripper find herself hopelessly in love with a pastor?

She closed the door and leaned back against it. She doubted she'd get much sleep before the late shift tonight.

# Chapter Eleven

A dangling string of sleigh bells jangled merrily when Luke pushed open the door to Whimsy, the little bake shop in town. Off to his right, at the far table, Brock Anderson waved him over. Tall, with dark brown hair and eyes, Brock looked the perfect lawyer in his gray suit and red tie. Luke strolled over and took a seat opposite him.

"Thanks for meeting me here. I only have a short window of time between clients, so I took the liberty of ordering you coffee and a cupcake," Brock said.

"Thanks," Luke said. "Very thoughtful of you."

Mandy Brighton, owner of Whimsy, came over carrying a tray laden with coffee cups and cupcakes.

"Here we go," she said cheerfully. "Two coffees and two specialty of the month, Jack-o'-Lantern cupcakes! If that's all for now, I have to go work on the cake I'm decorating. Just call out if you need anything."

"Will do," Brock replied. "It's usually pretty slow here mid-afternoon, once the lunch rush is over. That's why I picked this place. That and it's close to my office."

"You're at Anderson and Anderson, aren't you?" Luke asked.

"That's right," Brock replied, adding cream and sugar to his coffee.

"Who's the other Anderson? Your dad?" Luke took a bite of his cupcake. "Mmm. Pumpkin."

"That would be my uncle, Reginald Anderson. He'll be my best man, if I ever get married," he added with a sigh.

"Yes. Riley said there's some doubt," Luke replied.

Brock tapped his pen on the table absently, then looked up to meet Luke's gaze. "This is completely confidential, right?"

"Absolutely," Luke confirmed. "How can I help you?"

Brock leaned back in his chair, eyeing Luke critically. "To be honest, I'm not sure you can. You look younger than I am, so I'm wondering how much marriage advice you can give."

Luke chuckled. "Well, if I were to only give advice based on my personal experience you'd be in trouble. Fortunately, I have help from a higher power." He patted the Bible he'd brought with him.

"I already spoke with Riley, so I understand the problem as she sees it, but I'd like to hear your side of things," Luke continued.

"Let me guess," Brock said. "I'm being unreasonable."

"Something like that. She says you're forcing her to choose between you and her mother. It's either cut mom out of her life or the wedding is off."

"Oh for... I did not say Riley had to cut her mom out of her life!" Brock protested.

"Okay," Luke said. "What did you say?"

"I'll admit I'm fed up with Lilith. She's like a force of nature. She blows in and pushes everyone around. She changes what we want to what she wants. I'm sick of it. Riley is my fiancée and this is our wedding. I want Riley to stand up to her mother for once in her life and tell her 'no'," Brock said.

"I see. I've heard Lilith Hamilton is hard to deal with," Luke said.

"That's putting it mildly," Brock sighed and shook his head. "This is just the beginning. Now it's our wedding. What happens when she thinks our house isn't good enough? Apparently she's already offended my mother by insinuating *I'm* not good enough for Riley. God help us when we have children! I don't want this... this monster-in-law trying to run the rest of our lives together."

"So what do you see as the solution?" Luke probed.

"I want Riley to stand up for herself... for us! I'd stand up to Lilith for her but when I do she gets upset with me. I don't know what she wants. She complains about her mother, but when I try to step in and help, all of a sudden I'm the bad guy and she's angry with me," Brock complained.

"I can see how frustrating this is for you," Luke said. He sat back and pretended to think hard.

"I suppose you could just trade Riley in. Get a new girlfriend with better parents," he suggested, keeping his face perfectly composed.

"What?" Brock's voice rose. "That's your advice? Trade her in? What kind of counseling is that?" he demanded.

"Well. You're the one saying you can't stand the situation. Why *not* trade her in? What makes Riley so special?" Luke pressed.

"Everything!" Brock exclaimed, sliding to the edge of his chair. "She's the most sweet, kind, loving woman I've ever known! She's gentle, compassionate, and she puts up with me and my long work hours. Being a partner in a law firm can be very time consuming but she accepts my schedule. Riley's perfect! I don't want anyone but her. It's her mother I have issues with!"

"I see," said Luke, a smile tugging the corners of his mouth.

"What's so amusing?" Brock fumed.

"Did you listen to yourself just now?" Luke asked.

"Of course I... What do you mean?" Brock said, his brow furrowed.

"When you listed all the qualities you loved about Riley," Luke explained. "She's sweet, kind, loving, gentle, compassionate, patient."

"Yeah. I said that. So?"

"All the things you love most about her are the very characteristics that make it difficult for her to stand up to her mother," Luke said. "You're asking her to change her very nature, the same nature that made you fall in love with her in the first place. Are you really sure you want that to change?"

Brock sat back in his chair and glowered at Luke for a minute, then shook his head. "Damn. You're right." He narrowed his eyes, inspecting Luke. "You're pretty smart for such a young guy."

"Thanks for letting me have the opportunity to help."

"But now what?" Brock said. "I do love Riley, just the way she is, but the situation is intolerable."

"Give me some time to pray about this. In the meantime, I want you to write down what's most important to you when it comes to you and Riley. Write down your vision of your future together, but stick to what's really important. Leave out anything you could compromise on," Luke advised.

"Okay, I can do that," Brock replied.

"Good. Second, call my secretary, Delores, and set up a time when both you and Riley can come see me together."

Brock stood. "Yes. I'll definitely do that. Thanks, Pastor Dixon." He held his hand out.

Luke rose and shook Brock's hand. "Please, call me Luke."

# Chapter Twelve

Big Joe had seen it all.

He'd seen the college boys roll in after a day of skiing, drunk already and getting louder by the minute. He'd seen the divorcee cougars prowling the place, buying shots and picking up those same college boys. He'd seen the barely legal party girls with too little clothing on and the old drunks who didn't know when to go home.

Yes, he'd seen it all, including the two dingbats trying to fly under his radar. As if trench coats and fedoras would help them blend in. But what else should he expect on a Saturday night?

Joe slapped the bar as he passed and said to the bartender, "Keep an eye on the door."

He pushed through the crowd gathered near the stage, waiting for the girls to perform. He came up behind the two fedoras silently, and with a quick flick of his hands, flipped the hats off simultaneously. Two pimpled faces swiveled to gape at him in horror.

Joe grabbed each of them by the collar and rumbled, "What do you two foo's think you doin'?"

They stuttered and stumbled over their words as he lifted them to their tip toes and marched them off the dance floor, past the bar, around the corner and down the hall toward his office. He chuckled to himself at their moans of disappointment when the music kicked up a notch and the crowd started cheering to signal the start of tonight's performances.

He shoved them into his office and ordered, "Sit!"

Joe walked back to the door, closed it and leaned back against it, effectively cutting off all means of escape. At six foot two and 220 pounds of solid muscle, he never had trouble intimidating people. He considered it a gift. He narrowed his eyes at the two boys.

"Where's your ID?" he asked the first boy, a red-haired skinny kid that couldn't have been more than fifteen.

"I…I lost it. But I'm eighteen, aren't I, Kyle?" He asked his friend, another skinny kid but with straggly brown hair.

Kyle nodded forcefully. "Yup. Totally. Tyler's eighteen. I'll vouch for him."

"Uh huh. I feel so much better 'bout this now," Joe said. "So where's yo ID, *Kyle*?"

Kyle stuffed his hand into his pocket and after some fishing around produced a tattered looking University of Calgary ID card and handed it to Joe.

Joe looked at the card, then at Kyle, then back at the card. Then he laughed, long and deep, a sound that brought out the flavor of his homeland, Jamaica.

He stopped laughing abruptly and flicked the card back at Kyle. "You ain't no 35 foo! Maybe you think I'm stupid?"

"N-no," they stuttered in unison.

"Does yo' momma know you're here, trying to look at de girls? Let's give her a call and find out."

The two faces dropped.

Kyle said, "My mom's gone to Calgary for the weekend. She's out partying by now. You can try to call her, but even if she answers, she won't be home 'til tomorrow night."

Joe turned to Tyler. "What about you? Yo momma out, too?"

Tyler shrugged. "No, she's home. She was passed out on the couch when we left an hour ago."

"I see. Den we got us a situation. I guess I better call de police."

"No! Don't do that. Please, mister," the boys talked over each other in a rush.

"What I do with you den? I'm not gonna just send you out on yo own again. You find more trouble fo' sure."

The boys whispered back and forth a moment, arguing, then Kyle spoke up. "Can you call Pastor Luke, from the church?"

"You want me to wake up de preacher at dis hour? You crazy."

"Yeah. Please. He said we could call any time," Tyler added. Kyle nodded his agreement, looking remarkably like a bobble-head doll.

Joe thought a moment, then shrugged. He didn't really want the boys charged with a crime. He just wanted to scare them enough to not try sneaking back into his pub. He sure enough didn't need the cops to shut him down for allowing minors to be there.

"Okay. I call him. But if he don' come, I call de police."

* * *

Luke pulled his truck up in the parking lot behind The Wobbly Dog. There were no spaces available, so he blocked off a couple cars by parallel parking right behind them. He didn't plan on staying any longer than necessary, so hopefully he wouldn't get towed before he came back out. At midnight, he doubted the parking patrol was on duty anyway.

Luke walked around the block to the front entrance off Elk Street. He could hear the music throbbing from out on the street. In his mind, it was a different street, in a different city, with a different heavy wooden door, and another private hell. He stopped just before the door, and stood there, immobile.

Memories flooded back. He tried to shove them down, but to no avail. He didn't even have to open the door. It was all fresh in his mind. The smell of stale beer and vomit. The crude cat calls and lewd comments. The shame. He could feel the cold sweat popping out on his brow, could hear the blood rushing in his ears.

He reached out to open the door, saw his hand shaking. Then he took a deep breath, straightened his back, and opened the door to The Wobbly Dog.

The smell and sound hit him like a wind shear. He had to stop a moment to orient himself. An almost naked woman with a long blonde mane of hair was writhing sinuously on the stage. He turned away, not wanting to watch, trying not to picture that other woman, long ago.

Luke swallowed the bile in his throat and strode over to the bar. Let's just get this done and be gone.

"What can I get you?" the bartender asked.

"Nothing. Some guy named Joe called me. Said he had a couple of minors sneak in. I've come to get them." Luke couldn't keep his eyes from darting down behind the bar. He could still see the view. Peering past the bar, straining to see through the legs to the dancer on stage. The way the men treated her. His stomach turned.

"That would be Big Joe." The bartender pointed toward the door Luke had just come through. "He'll be in his office. Go left at the door and past the washrooms. It's on the left of the hall."

"Thanks." Luke turned back, avoiding looking at the dancer. No matter what she might look like, he would only ever see *her*.

He found the door marked 'Office' and knocked. A large black man with a bald head opened it. Luke found himself having to look up to meet the man's gaze, something he didn't have to do often.

"You da preacher?" Big Joe asked.

"Yeah. That's me."

Joe swung the door open and indicated the two teens with a sweep of his arm. "Dis is what I found, sneakin' into my bar."

Kyle and Tyler looked morosely back at Luke from their chairs against the wall. Luke folded his arms across his chest and glared back at them. Idiot boys. He'd had to come here, to this of all places, because they couldn't just stay home. He bit back a sarcastic comment.

"What are you doing here?" Luke demanded. Kyle sat staring at his feet, hands stuffed in his coat pockets. Tyler squirmed in his seat, picking at a hangnail. Neither responded to the question. Joe moved across the room to lean back against the edge of his cluttered desk. He glared at the two youths, his dark skin making the whites of his eyes appear even whiter. It gave him a dangerous look.

Luke glared at them, too. "Well?"

"We didn't mean no harm. We just wanted to watch. We weren't drinkin' or nothin'," Tyler complained sullenly, not making eye contact.

"Well, I guess that's something," Luke allowed. "But you could still get this bar shut down for violations. Then all these people would be out of work. I'd say that's harm enough, wouldn't you?"

Neither boy responded. Luke felt his teeth clenching. You wanted to help these kids, he reminded himself.

"Both of you! On your feet," Luke ordered. "You apologize right now to Mr. Joe here, and then you thank him."

"Thank him? For what?" Tyler complained.

"For giving you a second chance to be a good citizen by not calling the police," Luke explained. "Unless you'd like him to call the cops. It's up to you."

"No. We're sorry, aren't we, Tyler?" Kyle stood to his feet and tugged on Tyler's arm to encourage him up.

Tyler got slowly to his feet. "I'm sorry for sneaking in," he said sullenly.

"And?" Luke prompted.

"Thank you for not calling the cops," Kyle added.

"Thanks," Tyler mumbled after Kyle poked him again.

"Thank you for your patience, Joe. This won't happen again." Luke shook Big Joe's hand.

"If it does happen again, I be calling de cops first. Ya hear?" Big Joe glared at them.

"Come on, you two. We've wasted enough of his time," Luke said. He herded the boys out the office door and down the hall toward the main exit.

The crowd was hooting and hollering at the dancer as they came into the main room. Luke grabbed Tyler by the back of his neck and steered him toward the door, not quite preventing him from seeing the girl. They had just reached the door when it swung open and two of the biggest men Luke had ever seen pushed through. People cleared a path as the two made their way to a table on the back wall and took a seat.

"Whoa," Tyler said under his breath. "I definitely wouldn't want to mess with those dudes."

"That's for sure," Kyle agreed. "Look at the tats on that guy."

"Let's get out of here," Luke said. "Before there's trouble." He'd seen men like them before, and trouble was never far behind when their kind showed up. He pushed the boys through the door and out onto the sidewalk.

"Thanks for coming to get us, Pastor Luke. You're the best," Kyle said. He punched Tyler gently in the arm. "See, I told you he'd show," he added.

"Ya. Thanks, Pastor," Tyler said, giving Kyle a playful shove. "Did you get a look at that blonde chick dancing as we left? Man, she was *hot.*"

"I know, right? Wow!" Kyle agreed.

"That's enough!" Luke bellowed at them. He clenched his fists. "That girl is a person not a piece of meat. She's somebody's daughter. She could be someone's sister. Even someone's...someone's mom! How would you like it if that was *your* mom up there?"

"Aw, gross! Don't say stuff like that!" Tyler curled his lip.

"That's disgusting!" Kyle agreed. "Why would you even say that? Ew!"

"Yeah. Way to ruin it for us," Tyler grumbled.

"It's the truth. Don't treat people like they have no feelings," Luke ordered.

"She wants the attention, doesn't she? I mean, she's the one up there stripping," Tyler persisted.

"Maybe, but it doesn't matter the reason. Whatever it is she still doesn't deserve to be treated like an object. She's a person. Don't ever forget it! And don't be going back to that place again. You're not old enough and it's not good for your moral character! Now get going. My truck's double parked in the alley."

Luke gave them a nudge forward and followed behind as they led the way. He tried to breathe slowly, to calm his racing pulse. They're kids. Just kids. They don't understand the harm this does to people, to families. Families like his, torn apart by lust without love.

* * *

Misty flashed her brightest smile and waved at the crowd one last time before making her exit backstage. As soon as the curtain parted, her smile dropped. She grabbed her robe and wrapped it tightly around herself but couldn't stop shaking.

She'd seen Luke! He'd walked right in and looked right at her! The same man who'd called this place a disgusting hell-hole only a week ago.

She sat heavily on her make-up stool and reached for her water, managing to knock the glass over. Water splashed all over the counter and cascaded to the floor. Misty grabbed a handful of tissues and tried to mop up the mess with little success.

What was he doing here? At one in the morning on a Sunday? Shouldn't he be resting up to preach in a few hours?

Worse yet, had he recognized her? The thought made her heart race and her chest tighten. What would he think?

He hadn't come up to the stage. He'd gone straight back toward the restrooms. Maybe he hadn't recognized her. Oh God, please!

She still had to go back out there and pay off Marco and Frank. She'd seen them come in about the same time she saw Luke leave. Come to think of it now, he might have taken two young guys out with him. Maybe that was why he was here. It didn't change the fact that her secret might be out. She took a deep shaky breath.

Misty counted out all her tips. She'd been so busy watching for Luke that she hadn't played the crowd as well as she usually did. Just as she feared, less cash than normal. She added the money to the rest of the cash in her envelope. It was everything she could scrape together after her bare necessities were paid for.

No new clothes for her. No bling. No extras. Every single penny went in the envelope.

After pulling on her jeans and a baggy sweat shirt, she fluffed her hair forward to obscure her face as much as possible. What if Luke came back in? The idea had her stomach in knots.

Misty pushed her way through to the back of the room where Marco and Frank waited. Marco had a scotch, neat, and Frank had a beer as usual. Frank leaned back in his chair as if bored. Marco watched her approach like a cat might observe a mouse.

Having handed over her envelope, she stood waiting with her arms crossed in front of her and her eyes downcast.

Marco opened the envelope and riffled through the contents. He leveled a baleful glare at her. He tapped the envelope on the table a couple of times, eyeing her as he held his glass.

She wanted to ask how much she still owed. She had been paying every month, for almost two years. She should be almost finished, but he never told her exactly. His look was making her nervous, and she decided now wasn't a good time to ask.

Marco took a swallow of the amber liquid. "What's the name of that brother of yours?" He turned immediately to Frank. "What was that kid's name?"

"Robbie," Frank rumbled. He downed the rest of his beer in one swallow.

"That's right. Robbie." Marco leaned back in his chair and took a swallow of scotch. He eyed her much like a crocodile would have.

Misty shifted uneasily under his watch.

"How's lil' Robbie doin' these days? Maybe I should stop by. Say hello?" Marco's eyes narrowed and his lips stretched into a thin smile.

"He's fine. Leave him alone," Tessa commanded. "We have a deal, remember?"

"I *thought* we had a deal," Marco said, "But this ain't cutting it." He held up the envelope again.

"I told you. October is slow."

"And I told you what would happen if we didn't get our money," Marco sneered.

Tessa's heart lurched. She still remembered Robbie's face the day he came home early. The black eye and fat lip, the broken look in his eyes, still haunted her.

"Please," she begged. "I'll do better next week. I promise. Just leave him alone."

Marco stood and, looking down his crooked nose at her, pulled a twenty out of her envelope to drop on the table for their drinks. Frank stood next, pushing the table away from him as he did so.

"Til next week, Babe," Marco said, then shoved past her and moved toward the exit. Frank followed silently behind.

# Chapter Thirteen

"That's it, boys! Good game!" Luke called out to the group of teens practicing their free throws in the Harmony Middle School gym. "Practice is done for tonight. You're all getting much better. We have a real shot at doing well in the tournament next month. Anyone who needs a ride to church Sunday morning come see me."

Tessa walked off the court panting and headed straight to her water bottle on the bench by the wall. This was her third Wednesday evening helping out with basketball practice. Luke had thought having a woman help out would encourage some of the girls to come out but so far there was only one girl who came occasionally. Tessa didn't mind though. She was no star player, but she did okay, and it was fun.

She took a few gulps of her water and grabbed a small hand towel to mop the sweat from her face. Across the gym Dan O'Leary's funny lilting accent caught her attention. It was mostly Irish, but with an odd mix of something else. With green eyes and hazelnut-colored hair that curled softly at his collar, Dan stood talking with Luke. Dan was another recent newcomer to Harmony. He had offered to help out with the basketball team, and he and Luke seemed to be hitting it off.

Tessa smiled as she watched them together. It was good to see Luke connecting with someone. Luke must have sensed her watching him because he paused and looked right at her. Catching her eye, he smiled and winked before turning his attention back to Dan.

She sighed, felt her throat tighten and swallowed down the lump with another mouthful of water. He was so easy to like…make that love. It scared her how hard she'd fallen for him.

Her mother had loved her father deeply too, so deeply that she'd never really gotten over him leaving. Mom put on a happy face for the world, but Tessa had seen the sorrow behind her eyes. She'd watched her mother stay alone for the past fourteen years.

Would that be her fate, too? Loving a man who wouldn't love her in return? Tessa turned her eyes back toward Luke, devouring the sight of him, the way he moved, the flash of his smile, the dimples that came and went with his expression. Had they only met barely four weeks ago? It seemed a lifetime. She loved him so much, but he hadn't yet declared his feelings for her. Was he holding back, or did he not feel the same way?

Could he sense her deceit? She knew she should tell him, but every time she tried, her throat tightened up and the words wouldn't come out.

The boys were wandering off the court. Having collected and put away all the balls, they were now gathering their own belongings and heading toward the doors. Tessa took another big drink. Her face still felt hot and flushed from running, and her scalp prickled with sweat.

She reached up and pulled off the elastic holding her hair in a ponytail then hung her head upside down to massage her scalp and fluff out her hair. She stood up and shook her hair out just as a red-haired youth walked past. He stopped and stared at her a moment. She took another drink. What was his name again? Tyler?

"You look kind of familiar." He stared at her intently.

"Well. This is my third week in a row helping out here," she said, looking more closely at him in return. He seemed familiar, too.

"This is my first time here," he replied. "I only came 'cuz Pastor Luke helped me out this week."

"Oh," Tessa eyed him closely. Where had she seen him? Then it hit her. The Wobbly Dog! He'd been one of the boys leaving the bar with Luke last Saturday night!

"Whoa! Your eyes just got really big." Tyler peered at her closely. "I'm sure I've seen you around somewhere."

"Y-you must have seen me at church," Tessa stammered. She grabbed the towel to wipe her face again and turned away from him.

"Nah," he drawled. "That ain't it. I don't do church."

Tessa began frantically pulling her hair into a ponytail, her mind and her heart racing in unison. She glanced up and saw Luke heading their way. Oh crap!

"Maybe you saw me at the Thurston Hotel. I work there as a maid," she offered. She kept her back turned, making a show of gathering up her towel and water bottle and stuffing them into her gym bag.

"Nah. I don't go there either," Tyler said.

Luke was almost upon them. Tessa fought down the urge to bolt for the door.

"Maybe I just look like someone you know?" she offered, finally facing him again. Maybe, if she begged him, he wouldn't tell Luke.

Tyler cocked his head to one side, looking her over carefully. Tessa adjusted her ponytail.

"Yeah maybe that's it," Tyler conceded. "I dunno though." He squinted at her then shook his head. "You almost look like one of the girls at the pub."

Tessa laughed a bit too loudly. "Ha! Can you imagine? Me? Ha! No, not me."

Tyler chuckled too. "Yeah. I guess that would be a little crazy, especially with you and Pastor Luke..."

"Yeah... Crazy.." Tessa squirmed. "Oh. Look who's here. Hi, Luke," Tessa finished.

"Hi. What's so funny?" Luke asked, looking back and forth between them.

"Nothing much," Tessa blurted before Tyler could speak. "He thinks I look like someone he knows. Hey, can I talk to you privately?"

Tessa grabbed Luke's arm, leading him away from Tyler.

"Sure. What's up?" He followed her as she headed toward the gym door.

"Have you ever had to do something you really didn't want to do?" Tessa stopped at the door and pulled her jacket on. Maybe she could work around to telling him.

"No." Luke opened the door and held it for her as she walked through.

The crisp air outside smelled of poplar and pine needles. Her breath whooshed out in a cloud of steam.

"Never?" She found that hard to believe. "You were never in a position where you had no choice?" How could he ever understand her predicament?

"There's always a choice. Sure, there were times when I did things I didn't really want to do, times I went along with stuff, but it was always a choice I made. I allowed myself to do it." Luke walked close beside her to her car in the school parking lot.

"But what about you going into The Wobbly Dog the other night?" Tessa blurted. "You called that place a hell-hole."

"How'd you hear about that?" Luke looked startled.

"I-uh, a friend saw you there." Tessa stopped by her car and turned to face him.

"Well, you're right about one thing. That disgusting pit is the last place I wanted to go, but it was still my choice to go there. Two of the youth I'm trying to help snuck in and got themselves in trouble. I went to go pick them up and take them home."

"So then there might be a reason good enough for someone to choose to go to a place like that?" Maybe he could understand after all.

Luke frowned at her, looking perplexed. "What's all this about? You don't want to go *there* do you?" From the tone of his voice she knew what he didn't want to hear.

"Me? Nah. Don't be silly. Why would I want to go to that dive?" She forced herself to laugh.

Luke chuckled too. "You were starting to get me worried. Someone as lovely as you should never have to go to a place like that."

"Right. Of course. I guess I should get going. Morning comes early."

"What are you doing tomorrow night?" Luke asked.

"Nothing. Walking Otis. Why?"

Luke cupped her shoulders and ran his hands up and down her arms. "I know you're busy Friday and Saturday nights, so I thought maybe I could come over after work tomorrow, walk Otis with you, then take you out to dinner. What do you say?"

Tessa smiled. A date with Luke? Absolutely. "I say yes. I'd love to."

"Good. I'd better go back and lock up the gym. See you tomorrow." He bent quickly and gave her a brief kiss, but not quick enough.

"Ooooo! Pastor Luke!" a chorus of teenage voices called out amid hoots and snickers.

Tessa felt her face flame.

"Yeah, yeah. Show's over," Luke said and waved them off with a grin. "Go on home now before your folks start to worry." He turned back to Tessa. "Sorry about that. Kids."

She climbed into her old Vee-dub and watched him head back to the gym. Someday. Someday she would have to tell him.

# Chapter Fourteen

Tessa sat quietly lost in thought beside Luke as he drove her home after dinner. It had been another wonderful night with him by her side. He seemed to adore Otis almost as much as she did, so the walk earlier had been tremendous fun. Dinner afterward had been even better. They shared so many interests, and he was the easiest person to talk to. She could tell him anything, well, almost anything.

She looked over to study his profile while he navigated Harmony's narrow streets. His chiseled nose and strong jawline were softened by the curve of his lips. Lips so often smiling in her direction. Lips she longed to kiss.

He turned his head and caught her watching. She felt her face flush when he grinned and winked at her. He always made her feel this way, all hot and tingly and flustered. But did he feel it too?

He called her all sorts of pretty things; gorgeous, lovely, an angel. But in Misty's line of work you quickly learned that men say many things they didn't mean. Actions counted, not words.

Her father had promised to stay forever, but he didn't. Luke could say anything, but she wouldn't believe it unless his actions said the same thing.

Tessa frowned as they pulled up in front of her house. She wanted, no, she needed more than words.

Luke hopped out of the truck and came around to open the door for her. This had taken her by surprise initially, but now she had come to expect it. He always treated her like royalty. In that sense, his words and actions lined up, but she was ready for more.

He offered her his hand. She took it and slid out of her seat.

"Did you enjoy your dinner?" he asked.

"Yes. It was delicious." She squeezed his hand while they walked to her door around the side of the house. Otis barked his welcome from the backyard where they'd left him earlier.

"I had a great time too." He stopped on the porch and turned her to face him.

Tessa waited, looking up into his eyes hopefully. She watched his gaze drift across her face, then pause on her lips, ever so long. His head started to dip toward her, she leaned in, then he abruptly straightened and cleared his throat.

"I'd better get going. You have work in the morning."

Tessa's heart dropped. Not again!

She reached up and slid her fingers along the lapel of his gray wool overcoat. "Don't go," she murmured softly, peeking up at him from under her lashes. "Stay."

He touched the side of her face, gently caressing one cheek with his thumb. "I can't."

"Why not?" Didn't he like her? Wasn't she pretty enough?

"Because it would be too easy to stay." He tipped her face up to the glow of the porch light. "You're the most beautiful woman I've ever known."

"But you don't want to kiss me. You're not attracted to me." Her voice cracked. She loved him so much and he wasn't even interested.

"What? Of course I want to kiss you. That's the problem." He brushed a stray lock of hair from her face.

"Really?" she purred. Time to prove it. She reached up to her ponytail and slipped the elastic off. She shook her head, enticing her hair to bounce free in loose waves about her face, all the while staring up into his eyes. She undid the lowest button on his coat, then the next, until it hung open.

"Then why don't you show me how you feel?" she whispered. Starting at his belly, she slid her hands up the front of his shirt, skimming over his taut muscles and across his chest to loop up around his neck. She gazed up into his face and smiled to herself as she saw his pupils dilate and his lips part.

"Kiss me." She pulled him down toward her. Their lips met, and a warm giddy sensation pulsed through her. She heard him groan softly in the back of his throat, and felt his arms slide around her, pulling her tight against him.

Tessa parted her lips, letting his tongue dart in, tasting the sweetness of his mouth. She felt his attraction press into her, sending a warm rush of heat through her body. Maybe he did feel what she was feeling after all.

She moved her lips across his mouth as he matched her kiss for kiss. The heat built up in her. Her hands fell to his shirt and undid the top button, then the next, exposing the smooth skin of his chest. When she moved to the third button he stepped back suddenly, breaking their kiss, and caught both her hands in his, trapping them.

Breathing in ragged gasps, he said, "Tessa, I can't."

"But why?" She tried to pull her hands away but he held on tight. "Don't you want me?"

Luke tipped his head back and half laughed, half groaned. "Want you?" He looked her straight in the eye, his pupils still dilated from their kiss. "Darling, you drive me completely crazy with wanting you. I lie awake at night thinking of you."

He took one of her hands and placed it against his chest. "Feel that?"

She stared at her hand. Beneath her palm, his heart hammered through his shirt. "Yes." Her eyes flew back to his.

"It feels like it's coming right through my chest, and that's all because of you. I want you more than I've ever wanted anyone else."

"Then why won't you come inside with me?" Her voice sounded forlorn, even to her own ears.

"Trust me. It's not because I don't want to."

"I don't understand." Tessa shivered as the wind gusted around the house.

Luke wordlessly pulled her in toward him again. She slid her arms around his back, under his coat for warmth, and rested her cheek against his shirt where his heart still pounded. One of the buttons dug into her face but she ignored it. She felt him rest his cheek on the top of her head and speak softly into her hair.

"There are a couple of reasons. Firstly I'm a pastor. I made a vow before God to lead my church according to His ways and that includes waiting for marriage. That's what I hope the youth in my church will do. How can I expect them to wait if I won't?

"Reason two is probably more important to me. I've seen men treat women like carnival rides. They use them and then walk away when the ride gets dull. My... Someone close to me was treated that way over and over.

"I swore I would never be like that, Tessa. I respect you too much to just use you. I'm looking for a woman I can give my whole life to, not just my body for a night.

I'm going to wait for marriage first... I hope you'll be willing to wait for me too."

Tessa stood motionless as his words sank in. She felt her eyes widen in disbelief.

"Me? Wait for you to... Are you really thinking in that direction?"

"Yeah. I'm thinking about it."

Tessa stepped back to look him in the eye. Was he teasing her? "You... You've never said anything about that before."

Luke cleared his throat. "We haven't been dating very long yet, and I wasn't sure how you felt about me."

Tessa felt a warm glow sweep through her. He was actually serious about her. She couldn't contain her grin. "I think that I might, possibly, may be falling for you, hard." She didn't actually say the 'L' word, but she was sure feeling it.

Luke's answering grin spoke volumes. "Yeah. Me too."

"Are you sure you can't come in for a while?"

Luke shook his head. "Sweetheart, you are way too tempting. I know myself too well. If we start, all alone in your apartment, I don't think I'll be able to stop. Then I'll be just like all those men I've despised for years."

Tessa let out an exaggerated sigh. "Okay, but I hope you won't make me wait too long. You're kind of hard to resist too."

"You think so?" He looked very pleased with himself.

"Yes. Very." Tessa gave him a gentle shove. "You'd better leave before I change my mind and completely seduce you."

Luke took a step back, grinning. "That does sound tempting, but I will leave because I'm afraid you may succeed if you try. See you Saturday afternoon?"

"Definitely."

She watched him walk back to his truck. She could hardly contain the flutters in her belly. He was attracted to her after all. But marriage? She could hardly believe it. Her? A pastor's wife?

The thrill came to a crashing halt when she remembered she still hadn't told him about Misty. Tessa bit her lips, pensively. What would he think? Surely a pastor couldn't be married to a stripper. There must be a rule about that somewhere.

Tessa walked over to the back gate and let Otis out. He jumped around joyously, greeting her as if she'd been gone weeks instead of a couple of hours. "Come on, fool," she crooned. She let him into her suite, then paused at the door to stare down the road where Luke's taillights had disappeared.

She had to get out of this deal with Marco and Frank. She should be almost paid up after all this time. Maybe if she asked a friend, they could loan her enough to pay off the rest. But who had that kind of money?

Luke's face came to her mind, and her heart filled with such longing. He was the best thing that had ever happened to her. He was the strong, caring man she had always dreamed of. She loved him and couldn't risk losing him! She had to find a way out, somehow.

# Chapter Fifteen

"Hello?" Robbie's voice sounded cautious on the other end of the line.

Tessa took a deep breath. "Hi, little bro'."

"Tessa!" His breath whooshed out. "Are you oaky?" The note of worry returned.

"Yeah. For now. But I need your help."

"Sure. Anything. What's up?"

"I've met this guy." The most wonderful, amazing guy ever.

"Yeah? Do I need to bust his lip for you?" He didn't sound like he was kidding.

"No! I really like him, Robbie. More than like. I... I think I love him."

"Whoa. Serious?"

"Yeah. He's a great guy." She paced the floor of her dimly lit kitchen.

"So what's the problem?" Robbie sounded perplexed.

She hesitated for a moment. "He's a pastor..."

"A pastor?" he exclaimed, disbelief evident in his voice. "When did you get back to church?"

"It's a long story. The point is me working at the Dog isn't going to help this relationship any."

"Oh... I'm so sorry about that, Tessa. I should just drop out of school and help you pay them off. I'm a shitty brother."

"No. Don't say that about yourself." She'd lost count of the number of times they'd had this argument. "We already talked about this. If you drop out, Mom will find out, and we can't let that happen. Right? For Mom?"

"I know, but this whole thing sucks."

"Yeah… But if you could help me out a little, send me some of the tips you get waiting tables, we could get this paid off faster. Then I can quit and be done with it."

"Yes. Of course. I'll send every spare penny. I should have been doing that from the start. I just never thought it would take this long," Robbie said.

"Yeah. Me neither… Say 'hi' to Mom for me?" Tessa felt a pang in her heart. She missed them both so much.

"Come say 'hi' for yourself. Mom's worried about you. You never come by anymore."

"I'll think about it. I should go." She bit her lower lip.

"Tessa?"

"Yeah?"

"Love you."

"I love you too, Robbie. I'll see you soon."

Tessa hung up the phone, staring off into nowhere. She missed them being all together, but how could she look her mom in the eye and keep the secret?

It was impossible.

Her only hope was to pay off Marco.

\* \* \*

"It's perfect." Luke held the pale pink diamond solitaire up to the sun. He twisted it back and forth, watching the light dance through it.

"That's a lovely piece," the manager of Gold n Gems said smoothly. In his early fifties, slightly balding, with spectacles, he gave off the aura of infinite knowledge where gems were concerned. "Zero point three carats, light pink color, exquisite clarity. I'm sure she will love it."

"I hope so." Luke held up the sparkling oval in rose gold setting. "I'll take it."

"Will that be cash or credit?" the manager asked.

"Debit." Luke pulled his card out and only winced a bit when he okayed the amount. Tessa was worth this and more. He only wished he had more to spend on her.

Luke tucked the little velvet box into the inner pocket of his jacket as he stepped out onto Main Street. The sun emerged from behind a puff of white cloud, suddenly brightening the street. It seemed to him a sign of good things to come.

Maybe he was nuts. He'd only known her a month and here he was buying an engagement ring, but if this was what crazy felt like, he'd take it. He'd never felt so happy, so energized. With Tessa by his side he could do anything. She was the perfect partner God had made especially for him. He knew it deep inside.

They hadn't actually talked about it since the conversation last week on her back step, but she had told him not to make her wait too long. It already seemed too long to him, so why delay further?

Now or never!

Luke strode off down the street, whistling merrily. He was only a block from the Thurston Hotel where the love of his life worked. It was almost noon and he felt like treating his girl to lunch at the coffee shop.

He wouldn't ask her there though. He needed something romantic that she'd never forget. Now if he could just keep his big mouth shut until the right time.

# Chapter Sixteen

"Tessa?" The two-way radio squawked in Angelina's voice.

What now? Tessa picked up the radio and replied, "Tessa here."

"There's someone at the front desk to see you, *Chica*, and he's *muy* handsome!"

Luke! Tessa's heart did a little flutter in her chest. "I'll be right down," she answered breathlessly.

When she got to the front desk, Luke was standing there, waiting for her. A beam of sun caught on his hair, turning it gold, causing a halo effect. His stormy blue eyes softened as she approached and his smile widened.

Tessa had to hold back from running to him and throwing herself into his arms. After all she was still at work and in her green scrub uniform. What would management think? Instead she walked up and allowed herself to be enfolded into a warm bear hug.

She buried her nose into the hollow of his throat. The warm amber and citrus notes of his cologne tickled her nose. He smelled good enough to eat.

"Hmm," she hummed, then nipped him gently with her teeth, right at the base of his throat.

He growled softly, so only she could hear, then tipped her chin up and planted a quick kiss on her lips.

"Mmm. I wish you'd hug me like that in private," she whispered.

"Oh, my little sweetheart," Luke chuckled. "Like I told you before. If I were to do that in private, I wouldn't stop at just a kiss."

"And would that be such a terrible thing?" she asked, tracing her finger along the pulse in his throat and down the V of his shirt collar.

Luke snatched up her finger and kissed the tip. "Yes. When you've taken a vow to wait, it is. You are a very hard woman to resist.

"Let's go get some lunch. I have time to kill before my afternoon meeting with Brock and Riley, and I just had to see you."

"Sure. It's almost my lunchtime anyway."

Luke took Tessa's hand in his own and led the way through the lobby to the hotel coffee shop. Tessa curled her fingers into his, loving the way they fit, loving how safe and secure it made her feel, loving him.

He was everything she'd ever dreamed of in a man. She felt happy, just being near him.

Luke glanced down at her. He had the craziest grin on his face.

"What's with you?" She smiled up at him. "You look like the cat who ate all the cream."

"Nothing," he answered, grinning in a way that made her heart soar. "I'm just happy."

Tessa laughed. "If you're happy, then I'm happy too."

"After you," Luke said, pulling out a chair for her.

Lunch was fabulous as usual, but despite Luke's contagious good mood, Tessa picked at her food. He was amazing, so warm, and loving. She really could see herself with him for the rest of her life. And the way he looked at her? It made her feel like a princess. For the first time in her life she was seen as a whole person by a man, and not just as a piece of meat.

She had to tell him the truth, but how? He hated The Wobbly Dog. What would he think if she told him she worked there, and not just as a waitress? Would he still look at her with such affection in his eyes? Or would it turn to revulsion? She had to tell him sooner or later, but... What if he left her?

Tessa looked at her plate and poked at her salad. She had to tell him. They couldn't have a full relationship if she kept it hidden. But not right now. He had a counseling session to be at in a few hours. He needed to be able to focus on that and she was sure her news would throw him off balance.

She looked up at him and smiled. The warmth in his eyes as he grinned in return, encouraged her. Tonight. She'd tell him later tonight. No more procrastinating!

"Oh my GOSH! It really is you!"

Tessa jerked her head up at the unfamiliar voice. She had no idea who he was, but he was looking straight at her. A curl of dread coiled in her gut.

"Misty Dawn! I've seen you dance a dozen times," the man said as he headed her way. He was older, maybe fifty, with a balding head, a pot belly, and a big goofy grin.

Tessa felt the blood drain from her face. No. This can't be happening. Not here. Not now. She glanced at Luke. He was watching the man approach, frowning. Oh, God, no! He can't find out like this. Make him go away!

Tessa felt her heart rate surge.

"Can I have your autograph? Please?" Baldy held a napkin out toward her.

"I-I don't know what you're talking about," she lied, trying to appear calm with sweat popping out on her brow.

"Of course you do. You're Misty Dawn," Baldy insisted.

"No. I'm not," Tessa said, glancing wildly at Luke, then back to Baldy. "My name is Tessa. I work here at the hotel."

"No you ain't. You're Misty. I sees you every Saturday night, dancing at The Wobbly Dog."

"N-no, I..." Tessa stammered. This couldn't be happening. Please God, no!

"Look, mister." Luke stood to his full height, scowling down at the intruder. "I don't know who this Misty Dawn person is but *this* is my girlfriend, Tessa, and you need to leave her alone."

"No. She's not," Baldy insisted. "I don't know why she's being so shy. She sure ain't shy Saturday nights. But I never forget a face. She looks a bit different without all that make-up and stuff, but it's her. I know it!"

"You need to leave us alone, sir," Luke asserted.

"Look. See for yourself. She's the screen saver on my phone! Took this picture a few weeks ago."

Baldy turned the phone around and shoved his outstretched hand toward them. Tessa felt her heart drop out of her chest. There she was, hanging upside down from the pole near the end of her act.

"Th-that's not me," she implored.

And then she caught a look at Luke's face. He was white as a sheet. He reached out and said, "May I?" in an ominously quiet voice. When Baldy nodded, he took the phone and examined the picture.

"This is just a big mistake," Tessa said in a squeaky voice. "I get confused with that girl all the time." She laughed, a brittle, pathetic sound even to her own ears.

Luke stared at the phone for long, agonizing moments, then looked up at her, his face hard and his eyes glittering blue chips of ice. "So this isn't you?" he asked coldly.

"N-No. Of course not. I…" Tessa stammered.

"Then explain to me," he demanded, his volume rising with each phrase, "how it's possible, for this *woman*, to have the exact same birthmark, in the exact same place, with the exact same scratch through it, as you did three weeks ago!"

He knew. Oh, God, he knew!

"I-I can explain," Tessa begged. "It's not what you think. I…"

"Really?" His voice shook. He backed away from her, knocking his chair over with a crash. "Really?" he repeated, louder. "Because what I think, is that our whole relationship is one big lie, and that *you*, you're someone I don't even know!"

Around them, everyone in the coffee shop was silently staring at them. Tessa's heart fluttered in her chest like a dying bird and she could feel tears well up in her eyes.

"If you'd let me explain," she pleaded. She took a step forward, reaching out toward him, but he backed further away, throwing his hands up as if surrendering.

"Don't," he said harshly. "I don't need to hear any more of your lies."

"But Luke…" She reached for him again.

"No! Leave me alone… Get out of my life and stay out!"

He spun away, tossed Baldy's phone on the table, and strode out leaving a stunned silence behind him.

Tessa's knees buckled and she dropped back into her chair. It was hard to breathe. She closed her eyes and began to shake.

"So… About that autograph?" Baldy hedged.

"Get out!" Charity stormed up, pointing toward the door. "You've caused enough trouble here."

"But…"

"Out!" Charity spun him around and shoved him toward the door.

# Chapter Seventeen

All he could hear was the blood roaring in his ears, drowning out Tessa's soft sobbing behind him. He stormed across the lobby headed for the men's restroom. He needed privacy. He didn't want to implode here, in front of everyone, but he was about to.

Luke burst into the men's room, shoving the door hard enough that it bounced off the backstop with a crash. He shoved both hands into his hair and paced the room, breathing hard.

Tessa.

His Tessa.

Her naked image burned in his mind until it was all he could see.

How could he have missed it? Him of all people. How could he have been so naïve? So blind? The seemingly sweet and innocent love of his life had been dancing naked in front of everyone for months, maybe years.

Just the thought of it made his stomach turn. His beautiful sweet Tessa, just like *her*.

A faint, sweet hint of cigar smoke reached his nose. He ducked into one of the stalls, slamming the door behind him. That's all he needed. A spectator to watch him come unglued.

He was a pastor. He was supposed to help other people through their crises, not be the one melting down in public. He rested his burning forehead on the stall door, but couldn't slow his breathing or ease the tension building in him. With a snarl he slammed the heel of his hand into the door.

The tobacco scent wafted over him again, stronger than before.

Damn. Why couldn't he be alone for a moment? He braced his hands on the door again.

"You all right in there, boy?" a soft raspy male voice asked.

"Fine," Luke snapped. "I just need a little *privacy* right now."

"There's a pretty lil' gal out at the front desk crying her heart out because of you," the voice accused.

"*I* didn't do anything, *She's* the one who deceived *me*," Luke said.

"You ever hear of forgiveness, Preacher?"

"Look, buddy. I don't know who you think you are, but you should mind your own business... And stop smoking cigars in here!" Luke retorted.

"Maybe she had a reason for what she did. Maybe a good one. You didn't even let her explain," the man pressed on.

"What reason could there possibly be? For...that?" Luke demanded.

"Why don't you ask her?"

"No! I don't even want to look at her right now!" Luke snarled back. Who was this interfering know-it-all busybody anyway?

"You're being a hypocrite, Luke. Didn't you tell her God would forgive her anything? Now look at you."

"That's enough!" Luke wrenched open the stall door and stepped out, fists clenched. "I told you to mind your own..."

The bathroom was empty. Luke spun to look behind him, then left, then right. He turned a complete circle, but was all alone in the room. How?

Where'd that guy go? And how had he known about their private conversation? And what did it matter? All his hopes for a life with Tessa were in tatters. He clenched his teeth again. He had to get out of here, work out this anger before he did something dumb. The mountains. That was it. A good ride in the mountains would help him calm down. He still had a couple of hours before his meeting with Brock and Riley. That would be enough time to calm down. Maybe.

Luke poked his head out of the bathroom. All seemed quiet, so he ducked out and headed for the door. He had to get out of here, and fast.

# Chapter Eighteen

Tessa knocked loudly on the door to Mrs. Madeline Arbuckle's top floor suite before unlocking the door and letting herself in. After her initial bout of tears in Angelina's arms earlier, she had somehow pulled herself together and gone back to her cleaning duties, performing her job more like an automaton than a living person.

Mrs. Arbuckle's suite was always her last clean of the day, done around three in the afternoon. Today Mrs. A happened to be out, across the road at Whimsy, having tea with her friend, Emily Jamieson. Tessa scrubbed down the bathroom, stripped the linens and made up the bed in a daze. She shut her mind off, refusing to think of Luke, or her future now without him.

She succeeded fairly well until she was straightening up the sitting area after vacuuming. She paused to wipe off a photo in a frame. It was a picture of Mrs. Arbuckle and her husband, Walter, not long before he had passed away. Mrs .A often talked about him, and sometimes even talked to him, the poor dear.

Tessa picked up the photo and studied it a moment. Mr. and Mrs. A, both elderly, seemed full of life, joy, and laughter. The love between them was obvious, even palpable in the photo. It stabbed at Tessa's heart. She wanted a love like they had shared.

She had dreamt of it for years, ever since her father had abandoned her mom. She longed for a love that would stand the test of time, that would last until death or beyond, just like Mrs. A's had.

Tessa teared up. She had hoped, had dared to dream, that Luke would be her Mr. A.

Now the truth was out. She had been right all along. He didn't want to date a stripper. He couldn't even bare to look at her. Everything was ruined, her dreams destroyed.

Tessa sank slowly down onto the sofa, still holding the photo, while the image began to blur. A large tear splashed onto the glass, then another. She bowed her head, and just let them fall as she gave in to deep wracking sobs.

\* \* \*

Gravel flew as Luke pulled into the mountain parking lot of the cross-country ski hut. He shoved open the door of his truck before the dust had settled and unloaded his bike from the back.

Memories of Tessa, from his first sight of her in that same place, flooded back. Her wide easy smile and playful ponytail, the sparkle in her hazel eyes, and the lack of any make-up all had led him to believe she was the wholesome, innocent small town girl he had wanted her to be.

Had it only been a month?

It seemed like a lifetime.

What a dupe he'd been! He slammed his helmet onto his head, snapping the buckle together more out of habit than any desire for safety.

Luke slid his toes into the pedal straps and took off across the parking lot for the main trail head. Pedaling hard, he flew past the big fallen log where they had first trained Otis. The sunny afternoons came flooding back to him. Working the dog, laughing with Tessa, it had all seemed so perfect. She was perfect.

It was all he'd ever dreamed of. The fresh mountain air and pristine forests of the Rockies were about as far from the dirty, needle-ridden back alleys of East Vancouver as you could get. The fresh-faced, wholesome Tessa had seemed the polar opposite of his trashy stripper mom and her string of loser boyfriends.

Except Tessa wasn't different at all. She was exactly the same! The lying, deceitful little...

Luke rode hard, pushing himself to the limit, as if trying to outrun his own thoughts. He veered off the familiar trail he was on, and headed up a black diamond trail to higher ground instead.

Why God?

Why?

Of all the young women who lived in Harmony, why did he have to fall for Tessa? There were at least a half dozen young ladies at Winding River Church who had been batting their eyelashes at him until he started bringing Tessa. Why couldn't he have picked one of them?

But, oh no! It had to be Tessa. Rage surged through him, and he pushed himself even harder, pumping the pedals with all his strength until the sweat poured down his back and his breath forced like a steam engine.

The image of Tessa dancing naked burned in his mind, mocking him. Seeing that image had brought it all back. The horror and humiliation of a twelve-year-old boy surged over him once again. No matter how much he prayed about it, he could never seem to let it go. It haunted him always.

Luke reached the peak of the trail and started down the other side, quickly gaining speed as it curved back around the mountain. A thought crossed his mind that he should slow down. He hadn't travelled this trail before and didn't know it, but he shoved the thought away. Who cared? He raced downhill.

Tessa had lied to him, just like his mother. She was "working the late shift." Sure. Let him think it was at the hotel. It was no different than his mother claiming to be a waitress. What a crock!

He rode with all his might, pushing harder. He wished he'd never met her, never met either of them, never been born!

No sooner had the thought darkened his mind than the terrain changed abruptly. The trail of dry packed earth over bedrock widened to a steep gravelly slope. Luke's bike skidded down the slope, slithering in the shale as if on ice. He struggled to control it, but at this speed, and with no traction, the bike careened out of control down the hill. Part way down, the trail veered sharply to the left. Luke tried to navigate the turn. His back tire skidded out. He slid. The front wheel caught on a small log stabilizing the trail edge. The bike flipped over and flew off the edge, throwing Luke up into the air.

Mid-air, Luke pulled his feet from the toe-straps. He pushed the bike away from him and somersaulted, trying to land on his feet, but over-rotated. His shoulder hit first and he tumbled once, twice, down the hill to the bottom. He almost made it to his feet, rolling up at the bottom and planting his left foot to run it out, but that foot slid under a fallen sapling. His forward descent stopped abruptly with a sickening snap from his leg.

# Chapter Nineteen

Tessa sat crying on the couch for a long time. She didn't hear the door open, or the soft steps approaching across the plush carpet. She was aware of nothing until a woman's soft voice interrupted her.

"Oh my dear. Whatever is wrong?"

Tessa startled, and looked up into the clear blue eyes of Mrs. Arbuckle. Her pure white hair curled softly about her face, which was gently creased in worry.

"Oh," Tessa said, fumbling to put the photo down. "I'm sorry. I shouldn't be here."

"Don't be silly, dear. Sit right there and I'll have a cup of tea brought up. Or do you prefer something stronger?"

"Tea would be fine, thank you. But I really shouldn't bother you."

"Nonsense. No bother at all," Mrs. Arbuckle said. She called for room service then sat down beside Tessa on the sofa. Betty Jo, Mrs. Arbuckle's little Bichon cross, jumped up on the couch and pushed her way onto Tessa's lap. Tessa automatically began to stoke the silky white fur.

"What has you so distraught, Tessa?"

Tessa held back another flood of tears as she tried to compose herself.

"Is it Pastor Luke who has you so upset? I've seen you together at church, and here at the hotel," Mrs. Arbuckle prodded.

Tessa nodded dumbly, then sniffed.

Mrs. Arbuckle handed her a tissue and patted her back gently. "Tell me all about it."

Tessa poured her heart out, pausing only when the tea arrived, as if Mrs. A were her own granny. She even confided her desire for a love like the one Mrs. Arbuckle had known.

Mrs. Arbuckle smiled at that, then looked back over her shoulder to the empty room behind her. "Do you hear that, Walter? We have to help her."

Betty Jo stood to look, too, and barked once, wagging her fluffy tail furiously.

Tessa sniffed loudly. Poor Mrs. A. She seemed so with-it most of the time, but then she'd fall into the delusion that Walter was still here. Maybe losing Luke now was for the best in the long run. It would spare her the fate of Mrs. A, still trying to talk with her long-dead husband.

That thought caused a crushing pain to her chest, and a new flood of tears cascaded down her cheeks.

"Why didn't you tell him your problem sooner, before he had to find out like this?" Mrs. Arbuckle asked gently.

"Because I knew he wouldn't understand. He'd reject me just like...like..."

"Like who, dear?" Mrs. Arbuckle prodded.

"Like my dad," Tessa confided quietly.

"So you decided he was like your dad before you ever gave him a chance," Mrs. Arbuckle stated softly.

"Well, I was right, wasn't I? He bailed as soon as he found out, like I knew he would," Tessa accused.

"That's not really fair though, is it?" Mrs. Arbuckle said.

"What do you mean?" Tessa asked.

"Well. You let him believe you were a certain kind of person. You hid a whole different side of yourself from him, and now you're judging him for not immediately accepting it with grace. It must have been a huge shock to him," Mrs. Arbuckle admonished with a kind smile.

"Yes. I suppose so," Tessa admitted.

"Give him some time, Tessa. He's a good man," Mrs. Arbuckle coaxed.

Tessa stared down at her hands. "I guess I deserve this. I'm a horrible person."

"No you aren't." Mrs. Arbuckle patted her arm. "But you do need to trust him. Have you explained everything to him?"

"I tried, but he wouldn't listen. He wouldn't even look at me. He was too angry," Tessa said.

"He was upset and hurt. There may be things in his past too. You need to go explain," Mrs. Arbuckle said.

"He won't listen," Tessa insisted.

"Make him listen. Then leave it up to the Lord." Mrs. Arbuckle smiled at her.

"I'll try," Tessa replied halfheartedly.

Mrs. Arbuckle turned and looked over her shoulder again. "What's that, Walter? Oh, dear!" She turned back to Tessa. "Walter says Luke's in trouble. You need to go find him. He's up in the mountains."

"Mrs. Arbuckle." Tessa dabbed her eyes with a tissue. "I really appreciate you trying to help, but you do know that Walter passed away some years ago… Remember?"

"So?" Mrs. Arbuckle challenged. "When you love someone deeply, you can never really lose them. They are always with you. Now you'd better go. Walter says you need to hurry."

Betty Jo added a little yip as if to agree.

"All right. Thank you, Mrs. Arbuckle. For everything," Tessa replied. Poor daffy old lady. She was very sweet though.

* * *

The angry chatter of a nearby squirrel intruded into Luke's awareness, followed by a low moaning sound and a pervasive, agonizing throb that enveloped his whole body. It took a moment to realize the moan was coming from his own throat.

He cracked his eyes open, trying to get his bearings. He was lying on his side, looking out across a gravelly, leaf-strewn slope at the edge of a pine forest. He could see the wheel of his bike poking out of the underbrush a few meters away. It was difficult to see, and Luke realized there was a layer of cloud blocking what was left of a quickly sinking sun. Much lower than he remembered. So he must have been lying here awhile.

Luke rolled to his back and screamed as searing hot pain shot up his leg. He froze, drenched in sweat, trying to catch his breath. Don't pass out. Don't pass out.

When the agony ebbed back to a dull throb, Luke forced his eyes open and cautiously lifted his head to look down at the injured leg. A gleaming white piece of bone poked through a bloodstained tear in his blue cycling pants.

Luke let his head drop back and shuddered. Broken. Badly. There'd be no walking out on that leg.

What little first aid training he had reminded him there were some major blood vessels down there. Even if he could stand the pain of dragging himself through the forest with an unstable leg, if he cut an artery on a sharp bone edge, he could bleed to death before finding help.

Luke began to shiver. His cycling gear, designed for high energy performance, did little to retain his body heat now. A cold wind hissed through the trees, cutting through his clothes as if they weren't there. He wrapped his arms across his chest.

For the first time, he realized he'd told no one where he was going. No one, not even Delores. He stared up at the white sky, shivering. The mountain peaks, so beautiful on a sunny day, loomed darkly above him now like threatening monsters waiting to devour him. People disappeared in the mountains all the time, some never to be found.

Would that be his destiny? After overcoming so much in his life, would it all end so soon?

He closed his eyes. Tessa's face floated there. Would she miss him? Or would she be glad he was gone after the horrible way he'd treated her? Would she try to find him? No. She wouldn't even know he was missing until it was too late.

Something cold touched his face, then again. Luke opened his eyes. Another snowflake drifted lazily to the ground. Awesome. The first snow of the season. Soon it would cover the ground, covering any scent trail he may have left, covering his body until it melted again next May. He had to move.

Luke pushed himself up until he was half-sitting. This was going to hurt. He took a deep breath, and holding it, tried to drag himself across the ground. Pain exploded in his leg, still trapped at the ankle by the fallen trees, and surged through him. Luke collapsed to the ground as darkness washed over him and he sank into unconsciousness.

\* \* \*

Tessa pushed her maid's cart down the hall to the elevator and hit the down button. Poor Mrs. A. She was always so kind even if she was a bit loopy. Maybe it was the cigars. Tessa had never actually seen her smoke them, but there was always a faint hint of cigar in her rooms.

Tessa put her maid's cart and supplies away in the cleaners' storage area in the basement, then headed slowly back upstairs to the main floor. She glanced at her watch. It was ridiculous to think Luke was up on the mountain right now. He'd had a meeting with Brock and Riley this afternoon and he would never miss that. He took his responsibilities as pastor too seriously to do that.

Tessa had parked on the street that morning, and was trudging back through the lobby, heading for the door, when she saw Angelina waving frantically at her.

"Tessa!" Angelina said as she approached. "Have you seen Luke?"

"Ange. You know I haven't. Not since he dumped me this afternoon. Why?" The words hurt so much. She took a deep breath to keep her tears from falling again.

"The church secretary, Delores, called looking for him. He's thirty minutes late for his appointment with Brock and Riley."

A trickle of dread crawled up Tessa's spine. "Are you sure?" she asked.

"Of course I'm sure. Delores just called not five minutes ago. She thought he might be with you."

"No. I've been working. Sort of..." Where could he be? "Ange, give me the phone for a minute."

Tessa took the phone from Angelina and dialed the church back.

"Delores? Yes. This is Tessa. No, he's not here. Is Luke's truck there?.. No? What about his bike?.. Can you go check? I'll wait."

Angelina's large brown eyes were wide with worry as she met Tessa's gaze. "What's going on, Chica? You look white as a sheet."

"Mrs. A said Luke's in trouble up on the mountain. I didn't believe her, but now… I'm not so sure," Tessa answered.

"Dios Mio." Angelina crossed herself. "You better listen to her. Her husband's ghost tells her stuff!"

Tessa threw a worried look at Angelina while her foot tapped rapidly on the floor. Mrs. A's words echoed in her mind. *Luke's in trouble. You need to hurry.* What was taking Delores so long?

"It's gone too? You're sure?" Tessa asked moments later. "Delores, something's very wrong. I can feel it. Call Search and Rescue. I think he's up on the mountain. I'll go straight up to start looking. Tell them to meet me there."

"Angelina. Please punch out for me. I've got to hurry. It's starting to snow!" Tessa called as she sprinted for the door.

# Chapter Twenty

A fresh skim of new snow layered the ground by the time Tessa's car skidded to a halt in the cross-country ski parking lot. Sure enough, Luke's old red pick-up was parked there, alone.

She flung her door open. "Luke!" she yelled immediately. The only response was the chill sigh of the wind through the pines and the rattling caw of a raven echoing off the peaks.

A shiver ran up Tessa's spine. Where was he?

She flipped her seat forward.

"Come, Otis!" she called her dog out of the back, then grabbed her backpack full of first aid gear. She couldn't wait for the rest of the search team to assemble. A sense of urgency pushed her forward.

She clipped Otis' leash onto his collar and went over to Luke's truck.

"Suche, Otis. Find Luke. Suche," she commanded.

The memory of her last search taunted her. Otis had been following the correct scent initially, right up to the foot bridge that crossed the creek to the dog park. Andrew had been found by other searchers out there on the little island in the middle of the creek. But that day Otis had abandoned Andrew's trail in favor of a rabbit trail. Sure, they had done more training since, but what if Otis went off course again? If she didn't find Luke soon, the snow might obscure the scent completely. It might already be too late.

*Oh, God! Please help me find him.*

Otis cast around by the truck, then planted his nose to the ground with a loud snuff. He started out across the parking lot toward the main trail, head low to the ground.

He seemed intent, until a gust of wind blew over them. Otis stopped. Head up and ears pricked, he sniffed the wind.

"Otis! Suche!" Tessa tried to redirect his attention back to the ground.

Otis resisted, raising his nose to the wind instead. He changed directions, and tried to walk into the wind, away from the trail he had been following. Tessa pulled on his leash, holding him back.

"No, Otis. Where's Luke? Suche!" She indicated the ground again, but Otis whined softly, pulling in the direction of the wind. Tessa stood immobile, heart thudding in her chest. What to do?

Did Otis know something she didn't? There was no trail in that direction. Was he just smelling another rabbit? Around her, flakes of snow floated slowly down.

Oh God. What do I do?

Otis whined again, pulling harder on his lead. With a whimper of her own, Tessa loosened her hold on the leash, allowing her dog to lead the way, nose in the wind, while she trailed behind second-guessing every step she took. It was slow going with Otis cutting a path straight through the bush nowhere near anything vaguely resembling a trail. She navigated around trees and clambered over logs and through underbrush as tormenting thoughts assailed her.

What if she couldn't find Luke? What if she and Otis got lost too? What if she found Luke but it was too late?

What if this was her divine punishment for all her wrongs?

Finally she said, "Stop it, Tess! God won't let Luke die just to punish you. He will forgive anything if you're sorry. Remember? Luke promised! And God's going to help you find Luke in time. Just believe!"

She took a deep breath and continued, *"Okay. Help me find him."*

Around her the snow continued its slow twirling descent. Tessa pulled her touque down a little lower over her ears and then pulled out her phone to check for a signal. Otis was leading her around the back side of the mountain and she was afraid she'd lose contact with the cell tower that served Harmony.

Just as she feared, she was down to one bar. Where was Logan and the rest of the team? He should call her as soon as they assembled in the parking lot.

Five minutes further she checked her phone again. No signal. Tessa's heart sank. She pulled Otis back and stopped in her tracks, struggling with what to do.

She hadn't waited for Logan or the others. They wouldn't know which way she had gone, especially with the snow covering her tracks. She should go back to where she had a signal and call; but that would cost precious time Luke may not have.

She knew what Logan would say. He'd want her back in the parking lot to team up with a partner. That would use up another hour at least.

Her stomach twisted. What if Luke was just around the bend? On the other hand, Otis could be leading her on another wild rabbit chase.

"What do I do?" she asked into the wind.

Otis strained at his lead, whining softly. She pulled him back a step. She should go back and call. It was the sensible thing to do, even if it felt wrong.

"Come on, boy. We have to go back a bit." She gave the leash a gentle tug.

Suddenly Otis lunged forward, yanking the leash out of her hand.

"Otis, no!" Tessa yelled as he took off through the woods. Not again!

Tessa scrambled after him.

Stupid dog!

"Otis, come!" she called, then paused to listen. The forest had the hushed silence of new-fallen snow except for something crackling and crunching through the underbrush. That must be Otis! Tessa hurried toward the sounds in the gathering gloom.

The sun hadn't set, but had dropped below the peaks, giving rise to the extended twilight of the mountains. Tessa scrabbled through the underbrush in the shadow of a steep rocky slope. The snow was falling harder, making everything look white and making it difficult to see for any distance, but she heard Otis whine up ahead.

Something round appeared out of the whiteness. She stopped, squinting at it a moment before she realized it was a bicycle wheel. Her heart leapt within her.

"Luke!" she called out frantically. If his bike was here, he must be close by.

Otis whined louder, and Tessa climbed past the bike to find Otis in a perfect down position beside Luke's sprawled body.

"Luke!" Tessa exclaimed breathlessly, hurrying to his side.

She gently touched his face. It was cold, and his lips showed a tinge of blue, but he was shivering. Tessa let her breath out with a whoosh. Dead people don't shiver. She wasn't too late.

She grabbed both his shoulders and dug her fingers in a little, saying, "Luke! Wake up! Can you hear me?"

His eyes cracked open, and he stuttered, "You...
came..," through chattering teeth.

"Of course I came." She brushed tears off her cheek
with a clumsy swipe of her hand.

"Just hang on. I brought help."

She shrugged out of her backpack, dug through it,
and pulled out a flare gun. Pointing it at the sky, she fired
off one shot. Logan's team would see that for sure.
Hopefully, they weren't far away. She turned her attention
back toward Luke.

"You're freezing. What happened?" she asked, digging
through her pack once more.

"Going too fast...Crashed...Leg's busted," he
mumbled.

"I'll check that in a moment. We have to warm you up
first. Otis! Here!"

Tessa commanded the dog to lie beside Luke on his
far side, then unfolded a foil emergency blanket designed
to trap heat, and covered both the dog and Luke with it.
After fishing out a small flashlight, she lifted the blanket
again and shone the light down the length of his body.
The nasty twist to his lower leg and the bone protruding
through his skin made her cringe. She swallowed hard,
trying to keep a calm expression on her face.

"It's bad, isn't it?" Luke asked unsteadily.

"Well, it's definitely broken," she allowed, sliding her
fingers gingerly under his sock to feel for a pulse in his
ankle. "The good news is you still have a pulse here, so
you haven't cut off the circulation to your foot. That's
good.

"I'm going to let the team splint this when they get
here. I'll put a protective bandage over this bone until
they arrive," she said casually.

The truth was she wasn't sure what to do with the
jagged end. Should she splint it as is, or try to pull it

straight? That would hurt intensely, and she wasn't sure she could bring herself to inflict that much pain on him. Better to leave it for Logan than to cause more harm.

Tessa put a protective ring bandage around the exposed bone end and gently checked over the rest of his body before covering him with the blanket again. She carefully undid his bicycle helmet and removed it, then took her own warm touque off her head and put it on Luke instead. She undid her own jacket, and crawled under the blanket too. With Luke sandwiched between herself and Otis, hopefully they could warm him up a bit until help arrived.

She glanced at her watch. Come on, Logan. Where are you?

Luke's eyes had drifted shut, but his shivering seemed less. Tessa lay beside him, sharing her warmth, with their noses mere inches apart. Her throat tightened up. What if this was her last moment near him? She breathed in deeply, inhaling his scent, trying to memorize it in case...

She slipped her arm over his chest, trying to give him more heat. He opened his eyes again, meeting her gaze. She saw the pain there, and not just the physical pain, and knew she had hurt him. Her own chest ached within her.

She leaned in, needing to say how sorry she was, but not having the words. She brushed her lips against his, a feathery brief touch only. She hovered a moment, a breath away, and when he didn't pull back, she kissed him again, deeper, slower.

He responded to her touch, his cold lips warming to hers, parting and inviting her in. She felt her tears well up. Had he forgiven her? She needed one more chance to make things right.

His hand moved up, skimming her hip and up her arm to her shoulder. It was soft, almost a caress, and she leaned in deeper, but then he pushed her back enough to break their kiss.

"Tessa, stop." His voice cracked. "You're killing me."

"I'm sorry," she pleaded. "I'm so sorry. You have to let me explain. Please." She felt the tears splash down her face and brushed them away fiercely. It seemed all she could do today was cry.

"What difference would it make." He looked up at the darkness above. "Our whole relationship is one big lie."

"Not all of it. Not the way I feel about you. I'm sorry. I never meant for this to happen. I meant to tell you but..."

"Don't. Don't bother," he interrupted.

"No," she insisted, turning his face back toward her own. What had Mrs. A said? Make him listen? "You're going to hear this. You're stuck here until Search and Rescue comes along, and you're going to listen whether you like it or not.

"I don't want to be a stripper. I don't like it. No. Worse. I *hate* it. But I have no choice. I have to do it because I need the money. I can't earn enough as a maid."

"No one *has* to..." Luke started to say.

"*Yes* I *do*. Try to understand. About two years ago my younger brother, Robbie, showed up at our house. Mom was out, but I was home. He had a black eye and a fat lip, and I could tell he was scared.

"He didn't want to talk but I made him.

"He had been working at the casino as a waiter to help pay his tuition. He hated that our mom had been working two jobs to help pay for it. I was helping too, and he felt like he wasn't doing enough. He couldn't do more hours because of school, so he tried gambling.

"He's pretty good with numbers, and has a great memory, so he did well at first. A little too well. He figured he could pay for all his tuition and still have money left over to share with us.

"Then his luck turned. He lost everything. In a panic he borrowed money from some guys to try to win back what he'd lost, but he lost the borrowed money too."

Tessa took a deep breath. Luke didn't say anything. He stared up at the sky, but he was listening, so she went on.

"By the time he came home that day, he owed them fifty thousand dollars! He couldn't pay that much. That's when the loan shark sent two goons to rough Robbie up. They said if he didn't pay up, they would be back to break his legs.

"I couldn't let that happen to my baby brother. I couldn't! I met with them. We worked out a deal for how I could help pay it all back."

"I can't believe your mother thought this was a good plan," Luke interjected quietly.

"She doesn't know," Tessa admitted. "We couldn't tell her. It would break her heart. She worked so hard all her life so we would be okay after our dad left. She finally managed to save up enough for a modest apartment in the suburbs. If she found out about this she'd sell her home to bail Robbie out. We couldn't let her do that. It's all she has in the world.

"So we didn't tell her. That's why I left Calgary to come here to Harmony. The money's good during tourist season, and Mom won't accidentally find out how I'm getting it."

"By stripping," Luke finished, the disgust obvious to her ears.

"How else was I supposed to get fifty thousand dollars? I have no skills, no special training. Stripping was the only way to earn big, unless I became a prostitute. Do you think I should have done that instead?"

"No. Of course not. But…"

"But what?" Tessa insisted. "Do you think I should have let Frank break Robbie's legs? I couldn't let him hurt my brother. I had no choice. If you can't understand that then maybe you're not the man I thought you were," she finished defiantly.

"Well, you're sure not the woman I thought *you* were. How could you not tell me?" Luke retorted.

"I'm sorry. I wanted to tell you. I almost did. But I was afraid of losing you. I was trying to find a way out by myself so I'd never have to tell you," Tessa admitted.

"And how's that working out for you?" Luke asked.

"I know this isn't what you thought — what I let you think, but it's almost over. I've been paying them for months. I should be done soon, and I'll quit as soon as possible. Can't you just forgive me?"

"It's not that simple," Luke said. His voice was quiet, but held a hard edge. Even though she lay with her body pressed to his in the cold night, he still felt a million miles away.

"Why?" she asked, her voice small and frail.

"I came to Harmony for a new life, a better life. I wanted a wholesome, clean, leave-it-to-beaver life. I didn't come here to wind up in the same twisted family I tried to leave behind."

"I don't understand…" Tessa said, her voice catching in her throat.

"No. You don't," he said firmly. "You can't possibly understand how it felt, seeing your picture, seeing *that,* knowing I'd been trying to protect you from my baser instincts, trying to keep you pure, only to find you'd been showing everything to everyone the whole time. It brought it all back; the anger, the humiliation."

"Brought what back?" Tessa asked timidly.

"I was twelve all over again. Tessa, you made me feel like a fool. My mother lied to me just like you did. She told me she was a waitress. She worked the *late shift*. Sound familiar? And I believed her, stupid naive idiot that I was.

"Then one of the neighborhood kids told me the truth about what she really did. She was a stripper. I didn't believe him, didn't want to believe him. In fact, I gave him a fat lip for saying it. But I couldn't get it out of my head.

"So I snuck out the window one night and followed her to work. It was supposed to be only me and my buddy, Spyder, but some of the other guys met us along the way." Luke's voice had dropped low and flat, as if he were suppressing all emotion.

"We followed her to work, to the worst bar in town, and ducked in the back door when no one was looking. Everyone was watching the stage, so we slipped behind the bar and hid there, peering through people's legs at the stage, at the girls.

"You can't begin to understand what I felt when she came out on stage. *Her*. My... my own *mother*, stripping for all those disgusting drunks. I can still see it all; my friends laughing and pointing, the bartender grabbing me and hauling me up in front of everyone, my mother storming off the stage, almost naked, and slapping me hard across the face."

His voice broke, and he paused to take a breath.

"Luke," Tessa whispered, her heart aching for the little boy he had been. "I'm so sorry." She moved to touch his hand but he pushed hers away.

"Don't," he said. "I can still feel the humiliation as I walked home with all my buddies laughing and jeering."

"But you still love her, don't you? I mean, she's still your mom," Tessa asked, hopefully. If he forgave his mom, surely he'd forgive her too.

"I never looked at her the same after that. I felt nothing but anger and revulsion when I saw her. I started staying away from home as much as possible. She started bringing home creeps and losers from the bar. They were drunks, lazy slobs, some of them mean.

"I started running with The East Side Boys, stealing stuff, selling pot at school. It was only a matter of time before I did something serious. If Pastor Johnson hadn't gotten hold of me when he did, I'd have stayed in that gang. I'd be dead or in jail by now.

"I came here to get away from all that, to bury those feelings forever. And you? you've ripped it all open again.

"I thought you were so much better than my mother, but you're no different at all. You're just the same," Luke accused brokenly.

"I'm sorry, Luke. I…" Tessa's voice faded out. What could she say? He would never forgive her for this. He'd never forgiven his mother. Why would he forgive her now?

"Luke! Tessa!" Logan's strong voice interrupted her thoughts.

"Here!" Tessa yelled back. She slid out from under the blanket and stood to her feet. Snatching up the flashlight she waved it back and forth and yelled, "We're over here! Luke's hurt!"

Everything happened in a blur after that. Tessa found herself pushed into the background as the Search and Rescue team took over. Logan's strong presence was reassuring as he guided everyone's actions. Working together, the team released Luke's trapped leg, treated his injuries, splinted his leg, and back-boarded him.

Tessa watched from the sidelines, with Otis at her side. She followed behind while they carried him to a nearby open field where the S.T.A.R.S. air ambulance could land. The wind blew like ice through her soul while she watched helplessly as the helicopter flew away with Luke on board.

Tea, from The Tea Shop, came up beside Tessa and wrapped one arm around her shoulders. "It's going to be okay," she said. Her warm brown eyes were kind. She gave Tessa a little squeeze.

"Will it?" Tessa asked forlornly. Nothing would ever be okay. Not without Luke. She wrapped her arms around herself and shivered.

"Sure it will. It has to be," Tea answered, casting a longing glance toward Logan as he helped pack up all the gear. "It has to be."

# Chapter Twenty-One

Luke lay in his bed staring gloomily out the window of Calgary's Foothills Hospital. It had been a hard couple of days.

He had arrived two nights ago by air ambulance. They'd warmed him up the first night, and performed surgery on his broken leg the next morning. Since then he'd had a lot of time to stare out the window and think.

Tessa haunted him.

He understood why she'd done it now. She was trying to help her brother. But stripping? The mere idea turned his stomach.

Then there was her lying to him on top of it all. She'd said she was afraid to tell him, afraid of losing him. He should be flattered he supposed. But she'd violated his trust.

He'd prayed a lot in the last few days, but couldn't seem to reconcile his feelings for Tessa with his gut reaction to her job. To think he had wanted to marry her. He slid further down in his bed. He still wanted to marry her, fool that he was, but that was impossible. A pastor and a stripper? That could never work.

"Luke?" Delores poked her head into his room.

"Over here," Luke answered.

"Oh, there you are," she replied cheerfully. "I've brought you some clothes to change into. The nurse said you can be discharged as soon as you're ready."

"I'll need to buy some crutches before we leave. I'm not going to be walking far like this," Luke said in a dull tone.

So much for coaching basketball, or biking, or skiing, or any other activity that would normally cheer him up. He couldn't even walk now for the next two months at least. Why Lord? Why?

"Don't worry about crutches. I have that all taken care of," Delores chirped. "One of our church family has loaned you their set. I'll wait outside the room while you change."

The drive home seemed to last forever even with Delores chattering away beside him. Luke made noncommittal grunting noises every so often but didn't really listen. He stared out the window without seeing the snow-covered fields gradually morph into foothills and mountains.

His throat felt tight and his gut ached, but he wasn't hungry. All he wanted was to pull Tessa into his arms, smell her sweet scent, hear her soft voice, and hold her. That was impossible now.

They finally arrived home. Delores carried his things as he made his way inside, trying not to slip in the two inches of snow that had fallen. She fussed like an old mother hen, setting up his chair, finding a footstool and a pillow to prop his leg on and gathering some reading materials. He could almost hear her clucking. It would have been endearing if he hadn't felt so numb inside.

"You're awfully quiet today," she said. "Is the leg hurting badly?"

"Not too bad. They've given me good drugs. I'll manage."

"All right then," Delores continued, placing an apple, sandwich, and glass of water beside him on the coffee table. "Here's some lunch. I'll call Tessa and let her know you're home. I'm sure she'll want to…"

"No."

"No?" Delores looked confused. "But I'm sure she's worried about you. You'd best call her yourself then."

"Thank you for all your help, Delores. I'll be fine now," Luke replied stiffly. He slumped down in his chair.

"You're not going to call, are you?" she asked directly, hands jammed onto plump hips.

Luke shifted in his chair and stared out the window, refusing to make eye contact. "No," he said.

"I thought you loved her," she accused. "You've been raving about how perfect she is for weeks."

That's right, Delores. Rub my nose in it. "Well, I found out she's not the person I thought she was. Okay?"

"Is this about her being a stripper?" Delores asked bluntly.

"Great. Just great," Luke muttered and pinched his temples with the fingers of one hand. His head hurt, but not as much as this conversation did. "I see you've heard about her weekend job. I suppose the whole church has heard too?"

"Well… People love to talk. There were a few witnesses to that scene in the Alberta Rose Coffee Shop."

"So what you're saying is the whole town knows." He pinched his temples a bit harder. Awesome.

At her brief nod Luke dropped his hand and slumped further back in his chair with his eyes closed and face blank. "Am I fired?" he asked quietly.

Delores hesitated. Luke held his breath. She had warned him to slow down where it came to Tessa. He hadn't listened. It would be fitting if they replaced him with someone more mature. So much for all his big dreams for a life in Harmony.

"No. You're not fired," Delores said.

Luke felt his breath slide from his chest.

"Tessa called me yesterday," Delores continued. "She wanted to speak with the deacons. She told us you didn't know about her other job. We believe her. We believe you were acting in good faith."

Luke nodded briefly. At least he still had his position at the church. That only left people laughing at him behind his back to cope with. Well, he'd lived with that for years. What difference was one more humiliation going to make?

"Thank you," he said.

"The board is wondering what you intend to do now?" Delores said. She pulled another chair over and sat perched on the edge of it with her hands clasped in her lap, staring at him expectantly.

"I've already broken things off with her," Luke admitted, his voice cracking. He clamped his jaw shut and schooled his features to look blank. His heart raw, he wasn't going to fall apart in front of anyone else, not even her.

"I see," said Delores. She gave him a stern look. "Is that the best you can do?"

"Is that the best..? What were you expecting? Excommunication? We don't do that..." Luke stated.

"I was expecting the opposite actually," Delores said curtly. "I was expecting the man who claimed he loved her to show up." She sat back and crossed her arms over her ample bosom, staring at him over the rim of her spectacles.

Luke squirmed under her gaze. "I did love her. But she lied to me. She's made me look like a fool in front of the whole town."

"You did love her.., or you still do love her?" Delores asked. "Look me in the eye and tell me you don't love her."

Luke glared at her. Just say it! Say 'I don't love her' and this will be over. You can try again with a different girl. A nice girl. Someone you can trust. Just say it!

Luke leaned forward, meeting Delores' piercing gray eyes directly. *I don't love her!* But the words wouldn't come.

He threw himself back into his chair and muttered something very unchristian. "Fine. You win. I still love her. That only makes me an even bigger fool!"

"You're only a fool if you let her go," Delores said briskly.

"But she lied to me," Luke objected.

"She didn't really lie. She left some things unsaid."

"It's the same thing. She's just like my mother. How can I marry a woman like *that?*" Luke said.

"A woman like *what*, Luke?" Delores persisted. She leaned forward and pinned him with her gaze.

"You know…" Luke squirmed. Was she going to make him say it? "You told me yourself that whoever I marry becomes co-leader of this church. Plus, she'd become the mother of my children. How can a woman like that be a good wife and mother?" Luke insisted.

Delores glared at him. "You mean a young woman who is willing to sacrifice her own safety and well-being in order to protect someone she loves? That sounds exactly like the kind of woman who would make a good wife and mother!"

"But she's no different than my own mother!" Luke accused.

"Exactly my point," Delores countered.

"But…"

"Think about it," Delores commanded. "I'll be back tomorrow to check on you."

She stood up and put her chair back into place, then disappeared into the kitchen, returning moments later with his phone. She set it purposefully on the table beside him. Pinning him with a steely gaze, she said, "Call her."

He fumed silently as Delores let herself out and locked the door behind her. He watched her retreating back as she made her way down the sidewalk, toward the church.

He glared at the phone sitting silently on the table beside him. Finally, he grabbed the phone and pitched it across the room so that it bounced onto the couch. He snatched the apple next and took a huge bite before flinging himself back into his chair.

Delores could mind her own business!

# Chapter Twenty-Two

"Are you sure you're up for this? You look a little white around the edges." Delores stood in the doorway to Luke's office looking concerned.

"I'm fine," Luke said, brusquely. He grabbed some loose papers, tapping them loudly on his desk to even them out and then stuffing them forcefully into a file folder.

He wasn't fine though. He hadn't slept well since his accident. He hadn't eaten much either. The pain medications made him groggy so he had skipped them this morning, but that meant his leg was throbbing in time with his pulse.

"I'm sure they would reschedule later in the week if you…"

"I said I'm fine," Luke snapped. "I missed their last appointment. I won't miss this one. Show them in as soon as they arrive." Luke glowered at her and grabbed a few more papers to sort through noisily.

Delores straightened to her full height, which wasn't much. She pinned him with a stern look but said nothing, turning instead and quietly leaving his office. Luke watched the door close then leaned back in his chair and closed his eyes.

He swallowed the lump in his throat and tried to breathe. Worse than the throbbing pain in his leg, worse than the sick feeling in his gut, was the empty ache in his chest. He had never felt this hollow, this desolate before. The only thing that had ever come close was discovering the truth about his mother. That was nothing compared to this.

He thought of the ring in its pretty velvet box, tucked carefully in the pocket of his jacket. The jacket still lay in a heap on the floor of his room where he had hurled it before changing into his riding gear last Tuesday. What a fool he was.

A tap on his door made him sit up straight. He cleared his throat. "Yes?"

Delores poked her head through the door. "Riley Hamilton and Brock Anderson to see you, *sir.*"

"Send them in, Delores," he said. She must be really ticked with him if she was calling him 'sir'.

Riley stepped through the door first. Her pale blonde hair framed her face in soft waves. Her lips smiled but her eyes looked anxious.

Brock followed close behind, looking casual in jeans and a light sweater. Apparently he didn't have to work on a Saturday morning.

Luke held out his hand from his seat behind his desk. "Please excuse me if I don't stand." He tried to smile, to appear happy to see them, but his face felt stiff. Hopefully, it didn't show.

"Of course." Brock bent to shake his hand. "Riley and I were sorry to hear of your accident. We hope your injuries aren't too serious."

"I have a metal plate and a bunch of screws in there now, but it should heal up in time." Unlike his heart. That might never be whole again.

"So... Let's talk about you two. Did you bring the list I asked you both to make?"

Riley reached for her purse. Unzipping it, she pulled out a single folded sheet of paper. "I didn't write much down. Once I started narrowing it down to what I absolutely couldn't compromise on, it became a lot simpler."

"You too?" Brock smiled. He pulled a folded sheet of paper from his wallet. "My list is pretty short too."

"May I see them?" Luke held his hand out for the pages. Brock and Riley both handed them their sheets. Luke read each silently, then handed them back.

"Well? Now what?" Brock leaned forward, looking tense.

"Riley came to me concerned that she was being forced to choose between her mother and her fiancé," Luke said.

Riley nodded silently, her blue eyes clinging to Brock's face.

"I said no such thing," Brock stated, sitting taller in his chair.

A frown creased Riley's brow and her gaze flew back toward Luke.

"Hold up." Luke raised one hand, palm out. "I'm not finished. Brock was concerned that his mother-in-law would be interfering in his life forever."

Riley threw a piercing stare in his direction but Brock met it, unapologetically.

"I asked you both to write down what was essential to you for this marriage to work; only what you couldn't compromise on. Now I want you to read your list to each other. Who will go first?" Luke looked at Riley first, then Brock.

Riley stared at him looking much like an animal just before it gets run over. Her eyes flicked to Brock, then back to Luke again.

"I'll go," Brock spoke up. He hesitated a moment. "Like I said, my list is short. Actually it's only one word. The only thing I can't compromise on... is Riley."

Riley made a soft gasp and her hand flew to her mouth, then she laughed in delight. "Look what I wrote." She opened her paper and turned it to reveal only one word: 'Brock'.

Brock laughed, too, and stood up to scoop her into his arms. "I love you!"

"I love you too!" She fell into his embrace. Brock's smile was blinding and Riley couldn't seem to decide if she was laughing or crying.

Luke stared down at his desk so as not to intrude on their moment. He told himself he was being polite, but the truth was, their joy was painful to watch. Try as he might, thoughts of Tessa pushed into his mind, taunting him with all that he'd lost.

Finally, the lovebirds sat down again and Brock said, "All right. We've both realized what's important here, and that's each other, but we still have the problem of the monster-in-law."

"Brock." Riley scowled at him. "Don't call her that."

"But she is," Brock insisted.

"No. Riley's right." Luke turned his focus onto Brock. "When you asked Riley to marry you, you did realize she wasn't an orphan, didn't you?"

"Of course I did," Brock replied.

"Then you need to realize that you may only be marrying Riley, but she comes with people. She has friends, relatives… and a mother. You need to stop putting Lilith down. Every time you do, you force Riley into the position of either agreeing with you or defending her mother. In essence, you are forcing her to choose."

Brock scowled as he considered Luke's words.

"Lilith is a strong-willed, often overbearing woman, but under all that is someone who loves her family and only wants what's best for them. Try to see the good heart behind the difficult behavior."

Brock frowned, deep in thought. He glanced over at Riley's hopeful face, then back to Luke.

"Remember. She did do one really great thing. She created the woman you love," Luke said.

Brock looked at Riley again. His eyes slid over her features, then he smiled and let his posture relax. "I guess she did at that. I may just have to thank Lilith the next time I see her."

Riley laughed and clapped her hands together delightedly. "Thank you, Pastor Luke. I've been trying to make him understand exactly that. You've been a great help." She stood and reached for her purse.

"Hold on. We're not done yet," Luke interjected.

"We're not?" Riley slowly sank back into her chair looking perplexed.

"No. We aren't. You still have to decide who you want to marry." Luke leaned back, fiddling with his pen and watching her expression.

"Who I..? That's ridiculous! I want to marry Brock, of course." Her eyes flashed indignantly.

"Do you? Because you seem to value your mother's wishes and your mother's priorities over your fiancé's."

"Ha! Exactly!" Brock sat forward, looking smug.

"I do *not.*" Riley flipped back her hair with a defiant toss of her head.

"But you do. Are you having the wedding you want, or are you going along with what your mother wants at the expense of your own happiness?" Luke asked.

Riley bit into her lower lip with her top teeth. Her eyes flicked briefly over toward Brock. "Well…"

"She gives in," Brock stated.

"I see." Luke watched her intently as the inner turmoil played out on her face.

"Riley. You must decide. Are you going to marry Brock, forsaking all others? Including your mother? Or are you going to stay under your mother's thumb? You can't do both." Luke leaned back in his chair, watching her.

Riley's face crumpled. "I love Brock. I do! I want it to be him and me, together, forever… but it's so hard. Mom is so pushy, and she doesn't take 'no' easily. I don't want to hurt her feelings, but I don't know how to make her hear my 'no' without being mean about it."

"So do you always just do what she says then?" Luke asked.

"No. Not always." Riley shifted in her seat. "Daddy often steps in. He's the mayor, you know. He knows how to manage her."

"I'm not going to call in your dad every time we want to do something Lilith doesn't agree with." Brock thumped his fist on the desk. "For heaven's sake. What kind of man would I be if I had to run to my wife's father for help all the time? No way!"

"No. Of course not. You two need to learn how to handle your problems as a team. Outside interference will only tear you apart," Luke said.

"I don't know how to stand up to her on my own. It's just not who I am." Riley started to tear up.

"Riley. You've allowed your father to defend you, to be your champion as it were," Luke said. "How about allowing Brock to step in and become your champion? Let him stand up to Lilith and insist things are done your way."

"Would you do that? Without being mean?" Riley turned hopeful eyes on Brock.

"Of course I would." Brock reached out and took her hand into his. "I stand up to people through my job all the time. I've tried to do that for you before, but you get angry with me."

"Yeah. I guess I have. I wasn't looking at it like you were defending me. I thought you were attacking her. But I see it differently now." Riley smiled at him. Her whole face lit up and made her eyes sparkle. She turned back toward Luke, still holding Brock's hand in her own. "I could do that! I could let Brock be my champion."

Brock grinned too. "I can stand up to Lilith, no problem, now that Riley is okay with it." He stood to his feet, pulling Riley up with him. She laughed as he pulled her in for a bear hug.

Watching their joy felt like a knife twisting in Luke's heart. He tried to smile, to be happy for them, but he couldn't help but wonder how he could help this couple through their problem, but couldn't solve his own.

"We're going to have the best marriage ever." Riley pulled back from Brock's embrace far enough to plant a big kiss on his lips.

Luke looked away, schooling his expression to reveal nothing of his emotions. They were a nice couple. They deserved their happiness even if his was gone.

Brock held his hand out toward Luke. "Thanks so much. You've been a tremendous help. It never occurred to me I could choose to change how I felt about my monster...er, mother-in-law by trying to see her good qualities."

"Glad I could help." Luke shook his hand, then reached for Riley's hand as well. "Don't feel bad about your mom, Riley. A lot of people have horrible mothers."

She smiled graciously as she shook his hand. "I've never felt bad about my mom, only bad about hurting her feelings.

"She's really not a horrible mom. She loves me. She only acts the way she does because it's the only way she knows how to be. Sometimes moms just do what they think is necessary to protect their kids. I've never felt anything but loved by her, in spite of her bad choices.

"Thank you, Pastor Luke. I bet your own mom is so thankful to have you. You're going to be a great husband someday." Riley's face glowed with happiness as she took Brock's hand and headed toward the door.

Luke's answering smile froze on his face. Her kind words tore him apart. He watched them leave, and as the door closed behind them, he slumped down in his seat and shut his eyes.

His leg throbbed. His head hurt. He felt like he'd been sucker punched in the gut. On top of it all, voices from this past week from hell echoed back and forth in his head.

There was that old dude from the bathroom calling him a hypocrite and telling him to forgive Tessa. There was Delores' voice, asking him when the man who claimed to love her was going to show up. He could hear her saying over and over that Tessa was exactly the kind of woman he should marry. There was Brock's voice saying, 'I never realized I could choose how to feel about her'. Then Riley's voice, 'sometimes moms just do what they think is necessary', and 'I bet your mom is thankful to have you'.

Was she? He didn't know. He hadn't spoken to her in years. He'd never given her a chance after the slap in the bar. He remembered her face, though. It was so red. He thought she'd been angry with him, but maybe it wasn't just anger. He'd seen the same look on Tessa's face when the big mouth from the hotel had outed her. She'd been embarrassed, no, horrified. Maybe his mom had felt the same way.

At least Tessa had an excuse for her stripping. She was doing it to protect her brother.

That thought bounced around in his head for a while.

He'd accused Tessa of being just like his mom, but maybe it was the other way around. Luke sat up straighter, scowling out the window. Maybe… Maybe his mom was just like Tessa.

He'd always assumed his mom stripped because she liked it, and that she didn't care about how it affected him as her son, but what if she was only doing it *because* of him? She'd been young, uneducated, and alone when his father had abandoned them. Tessa had said it herself. How else could she make enough money to survive on with no education or special training?

He'd always thought she liked the attention, but maybe she was doing the only thing she could to raise a little boy all by herself.

He'd never asked her why before. He didn't want to know back then. But now, with his heart in shreds, it suddenly became very important. Did he even have her phone number? Luke picked up his phone and started punching in numbers. He waited, fingers drumming on the desk while it rang.

"Spyder? Hey man. How's it going? Yeah. Hey, can you do me a favor? Can you track down my mom? I need her phone number."

# Chapter Twenty-Three

Misty hooked her leg around the pole, held on tight, and leaned way back as she twirled slowly around it. The crowd's cheer was a dull roar in her ears, muffled by the thoughts screaming in her head. Luke was gone. She had lost him forever. Lost to lies and deceit and the best of intentions.

He would never want her back.

She pulled herself upside-down and, clinging only by her legs, executed another pirouette. Her performing smile felt frozen to her face, an icy mask to hide the empty aching hole where her heart used to live. The crowd before her shimmered in unshed tears.

She'd had no choice, had she? She had to save Robbie. He was her little brother; her only brother. She'd had no choice. Or had she?

She twisted herself upright and took a shaky breath. A tear splashed down her cheek, and then another. She swung away from the crowd so they wouldn't see, and continued her sinuous dance.

What if she had trusted Luke with the truth sooner? Would he have rejected her anyway? What if she had trusted God for a different solution? But it was too late. Luke would never look at her with love in his eyes again.

The ache in her chest throbbed deeper. She could still protect Robbie though. She would pay off his debt somehow, and shield their mother from the truth.

Maybe she should go work for Frank and Marco after all. Then maybe she could get this over with sooner.

Speak of the devil. She saw them push through the door at the back and choked back a little sob. Forcing herself to smile brighter, she pushed herself through the last of her routine amid hoots and hollers for more. All those happy faces and not one could see through to the pain breaking her heart.

*  *  *

Twenty minutes later Tessa wound her way through the crowd toward the back of the room and the two hulking men sitting there. She approached the table and silently slid the envelope across the table to Marco, then stood waiting.

"Your routine seemed a little stiff today, *Misty*," he sneered.

"Off night," she mumbled. Of course he would notice.

Marco peered into the envelope and closed it with a scowl. "You're short again."

Tessa dropped her head. "I'm trying. It's been a tough week. I'll do better…"

"That's what you said last time. I think maybe you need some motivation," Marco growled.

Tessa cringed back as Marco stood to tower over her. He reached out with his ham-sized hand and pinched her chin between two meaty fingers.

"It would be a shame to mess up that pretty little face of yours," he said, pinching until it hurt. Suddenly his eyes shifted past her face to something beyond.

"Let her go!" Luke's voice ordered. It was pitched low, so only the immediate area could hear him, but the command was unmistakable and resounded with authority.

Marco scowled and dropped her so suddenly she stumbled back a step.

Tessa swiveled to look behind her and her mouth dropped open. Luke, with a black eye and balanced on crutches with his left leg in a cast, stood firm, staring down both Frank and Marco without blinking. She'd never seen him look so fierce or so beautiful. Her pulse raced.

What was he trying to do? Get himself killed?

Marco must have thought the same because he stepped back and almost smiled. "Look, buddy. Seems like you didn't do so good in the last fight you was in, so maybe you should just mind yer business and get outta here before you get yourself hurt again."

Around them the crowd milled about, drinking, laughing, blindly unaware of the tension building at the back of the bar.

"How much does she owe you?" Luke asked.

"What's it to ya?" Frank replied. He stood up beside Marco, forming an intimidating wall of flesh. He flexed his right hand slowly. His knuckles crackled.

Luke didn't flinch. "How much?"

"Luke!" Tessa hissed under her breath. "I'll be fine. Just…" She stopped abruptly when Luke held up one finger toward her as if to say 'Hush'. His eyes never left Marco. He never wavered in his intensity. He held his ground.

"How much?" Luke repeated.

Marco scowled, his gaze never drifting from Luke's face either, but instead of arguing he reached into his front pocket and pulled out his cell. Looking down at it, he tapped the screen a few times, then meeting Luke's eyes again said, "Fifty-one thousand, eight hundred dollars."

"But... But..." Tessa sputtered, her voice cracking. She heard her own heart pounding in her ears. "But Robbie only owed you fifty thousand dollars when I started paying you two years ago. That can't be right. I've paid over two thousand dollars every month."

"Yer fergettin' there's interest. Compounded daily. Plus you've been short so there's penalties and travel expenses and..." Marco stopped when Luke held up his hand.

No, no, no, no, no! Tessa felt as if the floor had just dropped away from under her. She gripped the back of the chair in front of her to steady herself. She owed more now than when she'd started. She would never be free. Never. Her stomach tightened into a knot as the awful truth sank in. What had she done? She was trapped.

Her eyes darted toward Luke but she couldn't meet his eyes. What must he think of her? She was a fool to think she could get out of this, and he was here to witness her final fall. She was gasping for air as if she had just run a marathon, but could only stand there, waiting in a cold sweat.

"Fifty two thousand?" Luke repeated quietly and reached slowly for the pocket of his jacket.

Marco and Frank simultaneously thrust their hands toward their inner pockets too, and everyone froze for a moment. Each man looked at the others. Tessa couldn't even breathe. *Oh God protect Luke!*

"Easy boys," Luke said slowly. "I'm getting my cash."

"What are you doing?" Tessa whispered urgently, eyes wide.

Big Joe must have noticed something was off because he appeared silently out of the crowd and stood behind Luke's right side. Of the two, Joe was a shade taller, a bit wider, but Tessa's eyes were locked solely on Luke. His face was pale, but determined. His eyes pinched at the corners a bit. His broken leg must be hurting, but it didn't show in his stance.

Luke eased out a bank envelope from his inside pocket. The men relaxed their stances when they saw what it was. Luke offered the envelope toward Marco, then pulled back slightly as the big man tried to reach for it.

"It's fifty thousand even. If you take this, then it's over. Tessa and Robbie are free and clear. Agreed?"

"Why are you sticking your nose in here?" Frank asked, eyeing the envelope suspiciously.

"Look. Do you want your money or do you want to keep driving up here into the mountains every week? You know your boss will be pleased if you walk in with this. Fifty thousand. Right here, right now. Yes or no?" Luke pressed.

"Fifty thousand?" Tessa gasped. She couldn't believe what she was hearing. "Where did you get fifty thousand?"

Luke glanced at her briefly, before turning his attention back to Marco. He answered her question anyway. "The church has a building fund. I talked to the deacons and they all agreed that this was an emergency and I could borrow the money from the fund."

Marco scowled. "Church fund? What are you? Some kind of preacher or something?"

"Yeah. Something like that. But today we're businessmen. And you're being offered a buyout. Do we have a deal or not?"

Luke offered the money again and Marco took the envelope. He opened it, pulled the cash part way out, and riffled through it. Marco looked at Frank, who gave a brief nod.

"Okay. I'll take your money," Marco said finally. "I'll tell my boss."

"I don't want to see either of you in Harmony again. Understand?" Luke stated firmly.

"No!" Marco snarled back, suddenly enraged. "I don't take orders from no preacher. See? It's over if I say it's over."

Tessa's heart lurched in her chest as Marco took a threatening step forward. Big Joe uncrossed his arms, readying for a fight, poised on the balls of his feet. Tessa's eyes were glued to Luke, who was still balanced on his crutches and no match for Marco even with Big Joe at his side. Luke didn't waver. He didn't back down, didn't even flinch. Marco hesitated.

"Tonight," Luke said in an ominously quiet voice, "I'm not just a preacher. Tonight I'm still one of the East Side Boys and I still have connections. Should I tell the old man you want words with him?"

Tessa watched the color fade from Marco's face. "East Side Boys? From Vancouver?" He took a step back, frowning.

"That's them. You want to tell them something? Or are you going to take your money and go?"

"How you gonna tell him anything if you never make it home tonight?" Marco threatened.

Tessa's heart was racing. They couldn't win this fight. Luke was going to get hurt, or worse and it was all her fault. She should never have told him. She looked at him and was surprised to see a grim half-smile on his face. Glancing at Marco, it was apparent he found the half-smile disconcerting too.

"I don't have to tell him anything," Luke responded, patting his chest pocket with one hand. "I got my buddy, Spyder, on the phone listening to this whole conversation. He'll tell the old man everything for me."

Marco glared furiously at Luke until Frank nudged him. "Let's go," he rumbled. "We got our cash. I don't like this dumpy little town anyway."

Marco looked at Luke, then Tessa, glowering, trying to make up his mind. Finally he said, "We're done here. See ya around, babe." He eased past Luke and, followed closely by Frank, headed out the door into the night.

Tessa's breath exploded from her chest and her shoulders sagged. They were gone. Finally. Gone. She wanted to cry, or laugh, or she wasn't sure. With shaking hands, she brushed the hair back off her face and took a few deep breaths.

Something wasn't right. She looked back and realized Luke hadn't moved. He was still standing there. She turned toward him.

"Fifty thousand dollars?" she asked incredulously. "You borrowed fifty thousand dollars? To help me?" She could barely say it let alone believe it.

"Yes," he answered quietly.

"I'll pay you back. I promise," she vowed. Why wasn't he looking at her? Was he sorry he'd done it? That was so much money.

"Okay," he said. "Write me an I.O.U. Get Joe to witness it."

"What? Really?" Her chest tightened again.

"Is that really necessary, Pastor Luke? Tessa be good for it," Big Joe said sadly.

Luke just nodded silently.

An I.O.U. Tessa felt the sting of it like a slap to the face. He didn't trust her. She had to write it out for him. It hurt. But she deserved it, didn't she? She'd lied to him. Held back the truth. The one person who had loved her so deeply.

She blinked back her tears and sat at the table. "Just give me a notepad, Jo-Jo." Keeping her face averted she held her hand out to Big Joe who turned and took one from the nearest server. He handed it to Tessa. She tore off a page and quickly wrote out an I.O.U. and signed it. Joe leaned over and added his name to the page.

Tessa sat, staring at the floor. Finally, free from the stripping and the two goons who had haunted her for so long, and yet she felt no happiness. Even knowing Robbie was safe brought her no joy. Luke despised her and that was all that mattered. She took a deep, shuddering breath.

"Now give me the paper," Luke said quietly.

Tessa stood slowly, and took two small steps toward him. With her lip trembling, and her hand shaking, she offered the paper.

He took it gently from her hand. "You no longer owe fifty thousand dollars to that loan shark. You owe it to me. I've bought it. Now I hold the debt."

Tessa's head hung low. She nodded her understanding. She closed her eyes tightly to keep back the tears sniffing loudly instead.

Then she heard the paper tear. She opened her eyes and frowned, confused. The paper ripped again. She looked up and watched Luke tear the layers yet again. What? He put them together, and tore them one last time. Then, in disbelief, she saw him open his hand and let the tiny pieces fall like confetti to the floor. Her mouth dropped and she finally met his eyes, deep and calm as a mountain lake.

"I forgive the debt. You owe me nothing," he said softly.

Inside her, something cracked. Luke dropped one crutch, opening his arm wide and she fell into his embrace, wrapping her arms tightly around him and sobbing into his chest. He held her close, resting his cheek on top of her head.

"Why? Why would you do that?" she managed to ask between sobs.

"Because I love you, silly girl," he murmured into her hair.

She hung on even tighter and half-sobbing, half-laughing, managed to say, "I love you too. So much!"

"Sweetheart?" he asked after a moment.

"What?"

"Can we sit down before I fall down?"

Big Joe laughed and pushed a chair over. "No problem, Preacher. Dat I have a solution for."

# Chapter Twenty-Four

Tessa knelt by Luke's chair, her hand on his thigh. "Are you all right? You're white as a sheet."

"Give me a minute. It's been a long week." He lowered his crutches to the floor beside him and leaned back.

"Tell me about it." She smiled through the remnants of tears on her cheeks. "Joe. Can you please get Luke something warm to drink?"

"Sure dat." Big Joe whistled sharply, catching the attention of every waitress in the place. He pointed to the closest girl, and motioned her over with a flick of his fingers. She took his order and scurried off to the kitchen.

Tessa turned back to Luke. "You were amazing. I… I don't know what to say."

Luke caressed her cheek with one hand. "Say you'll forgive me for being such an ass."

"Me? But I'm the one who was stripping, and lied to you and…"

"Shh," he said softly, placing a finger on her lips. "It took me awhile to figure it out, but I understand now. If I hadn't been such a jerk I'd have let you explain it all in the coffee shop. So… will you forgive me for being a judgmental jerk?"

Tessa nodded through her tears. "If you'll forgive me for not telling you sooner."

"Already done."

"I can't believe how brave you were. I was so scared, but you stood up to those goons like you owned them."

Luke chuckled. "Yeah, well, looks can be deceiving. I was shaking on the inside. Who was the huge tattooed guy?"

"That's Frank. The leader is Marco. It's a good thing your friend, Spyder, was listening in. That was smart of you."

"Yeah. About that." Luke rubbed the back of his neck with one hand. "I was bluffing. There was no one on the phone."

"You lied?" Tessa's jaw dropped in a grin. "And you a pastor."

Luke grinned back. "I had to say something. There was no way I was going to win any kind of fight. So I bluffed. That's the first rule of surviving the street. Never let them see your hand."

"But Spyder's still part of the gang?" Tessa stood up from her spot on the floor beside him and pulled a chair over to sit on and another to prop Luke's injured leg on.

"No. After I got saved, he's the first person I pulled out of the gang with me. Spyder still lives in Vancouver, but he works as a counsellor in a drug rehab center."

"So you have no gang connections at all?"

Luke shook his head. "Not anymore."

A waitress came up with a frothy brown steaming drink and put it on the table beside them.

"Thanks." Luke smiled at her. "Man. I'm wiped." He lifted the mug and swallowed several large gulps as Big Joe came back over.

"This is different." Luke lifted his glass, eyeing it.

"Do you like it?" Big Joe asked, his eyes twinkling. "I call it Jamaican Cow."

"Yeah." Luke took a couple more swallows.

"Slow down, mon. Dat's gonna hit you hard if you drink it too fast."

Luke lowered his glass, eyeing Joe apprehensively. "What's in this?"

"Dat's my best Jamaican rum, mon! What you think?"

Luke set the almost empty mug on the table and rubbed his face with his palm. Tessa started to giggle.

"You didn't say this was alcoholic." Luke shook his head, starting to laugh in spite of himself.

"This is a bar, remember." Tessa shook her head. "Look at you. You look like you can't even see straight."

Luke smiled sleepily up at her. "I can't." He looked blearily around the room. "I probably shouldn't have drunk that stuff while taking those pain pills."

"Uh-oh" Tessa looked hopelessly at Big Joe.

"Don' worry. I help you get him to the car." Big Joe grinned at her. "I'm jus' glad I don' have to put up with those fellas in my bar no more. Dis is a good day!"

\* \* \*

Tessa awoke the next morning, wrapped in a blanket on Luke's couch, with the man himself poking her with a crutch.

"Wake up, sleepyhead." He gave her another gentle poke.

"You should talk," she mumbled, pushing herself into a sitting position. She rubbed her face then eyed him up and down. His hair was still damp, so he must have showered, but he still had dark smudges under his eyes and a fading bruise across his cheek. "I've seen you look better. I love how you're rocking the old, faded sweat suit look, though."

Luke chuckled. "These are the only pants I can get over this boot cast. I might not look it, but I'm feeling much better today. Last night was the first good sleep I've had since the accident. Funny thing is, I don't remember how I got home."

"You had help." She ran a hand through her hair and frowned. "Why are you all up and dressed? What time is it?"

"It's ten. I'd have woken you sooner if I'd known you were sleeping on my couch. You still have time for a shower before church if you want one."

"Church?" Tessa's stomach clenched. "But... but they must have heard about... I don't know if I should... What if they...?"

Luke turned and sat on the edge of the couch beside her. He took her hand in his and lifted it to his lips. "You're going to have to face people eventually. Better get it over with. Pastor Carmichael is here filling in for me this week. I want to go hear him speak, and I want you by my side."

"I have nothing to wear but my sweats from last night." She couldn't face them. They would hate her for sure.

"Like I said. There's time if you hurry. I'll drop you at home and go get some coffee and donuts while you get ready, then pick you up again. What do you say?"

Tessa met his gaze, sheer dread eating away at her. He smiled at her with such confidence. She swallowed the lump in her throat. "Okay."

If she was going to be with him, she had to start trusting both him and God. For better or worse, she'd go with him.

* * *

Tessa held the church door open for Luke to navigate through on his crutches. People greeted him as soon as he entered, but then a general hush fell in the lobby as Tessa walked in behind him. Tessa clutched her purse in front of her, feeling like a bug under a microscope.

Delores spotted them and immediately bustled over, enveloping Tessa in a warm hug. "It's so good to see you again. Now don't you worry about a thing. It will all work out. You'll see."

"How does she do that?" Tessa whispered to Luke. "It's like she can read your mind."

"Sometimes I think she can," he whispered back. "Come on. Let's go sit."

Tessa followed Luke down the aisle. She scanned the crowd and finally found the face she was looking for. Angelina was here!

She had frantically called her best friend from home and begged her to come. She needed her here, just in case things didn't go well. Surprisingly, Guy Lafontaine, Thurston's prized chef, sat in the seat beside Angelina. Tessa's eyebrows rose a fraction. How interesting.

Pastor Carmichael greeted them before the service began, then things proceeded as usual. Tessa tried to pay attention, but she couldn't keep her thoughts from straying. She felt like every eye in the place was boring into the back of her head. No one would ever forget this. She was crazy to have come.

Luke might think he was in love with her now, but after a while, he'd see she would never be accepted in his life.

"Before we finish," Pastor Carmichael said, "Pastor Dixon would like to say something."

Tessa's head popped up from where she'd been studying her fingernails.

Luke crutched up the few steps to the podium and shook the other pastor's hand. "Thank you for showing up on short notice to fill in for me."

"My pleasure." Pastor Carmichael smiled warmly. "Always happy to help out when needed."

"I may have need of you again in a couple of months. Will someone bring me a chair?"

Kyle, one of the boys she remembered from basketball, ran up with a chair and placed it beside Luke. Luke remained standing as he watched Pastor Carmichael make his way back to his seat, then turned to face his congregation.

A hush fell on the room. Tessa locked her eyes on Luke. The black eye was starting to fade into a shade of green, and the weariness had lessened. He caught her eye and winked.

"Thank you for all your prayers on my behalf. I'm doing much better and appreciate all of your concern." He stopped to clear his throat.

"Tessa. Will you please come up here with me?"

Tessa felt her heart race. What was he doing? She stood hesitantly to her feet. Luke smiled encouragingly, and beckoned her closer. She walked up the steps, and slowly turned to face the church while the butterflies darted around in her belly. Every eye seemed to be on her.

Luke balanced on his good leg and slipped his right arm around her shoulders pulling her close. "I'm sure many of you have heard rumors about our Tessa by now. Some of them may be true, but things are often not what they appear on the surface."

A general murmur arose from the congregation. Tessa stared at the floor. Slowly the room quietened.

"Tessa may choose to share her story with you some day, but for now please understand this. I know the truth about this woman. She is a good, kind, and brave person who did what was necessary to save someone she loves. No man could hope to find better. She loves God… and I love her."

More murmurs erupted.

Luke turned Tessa to face him. He tipped her chin up until she met his eyes. They were warm and smiling. Her heart lifted.

"You are the best thing that has ever happened to me. I knew, from the first moment I saw you, that God had brought you to me."

Tessa's eyes widened. What was happening?

Luke sat down in the chair beside him, dropped his crutch to the floor, and reached into his jacket pocket.

"Tessa Peters," he said formally, pulling a small velvet box from his pocket. "Will you do me the honor," he continued, flipping open the box, revealing a sparkling pink diamond ring, "of becoming my wife?"

Tessa gasped and her hands flew to her mouth. The whole church fell silent. Her vision began to blur as the tears welled. Yes, yes, yes! But she hesitated.

She glanced out at the people, all watching in silence, then back to Luke, who sat waiting. Would the church accept her? Or would they fire him? She didn't want to be the cause of him losing his position here. She looked nervously out at the people.

Delores stood to her feet. Slowly, loudly, she began to clap. Pastor Carmichael stood to join her, then Angelina and Guy, and soon every person in the church was applauding.

Tessa couldn't believe her eyes. She turned back to Luke, still waiting, but looking anxious. She laughed in delight. "Yes! Yes, yes, yes! I will marry you." She held out a trembling left hand.

Luke smiled broadly and slipped the ring onto her finger, then pushed himself up to face her. "You had me worried for a minute there, girl."

Tessa laughed and Luke pulled her in for a brief kiss. Around them, the church erupted into cheers.

\* \* \*

Angelina pushed her way through the crowd to where Tessa stood by Luke's chair, accepting people's congratulations. "*Chica!* I can't believe it!" She wrapped her arms around Tessa in a bear hug.

Tessa laughed, returning her hug. "I can barely believe it, too." She looked down at Luke sitting beside her.

"Did he really pay off a gangster to save you?" Angelina's eyes were wide with wonder.

"Something like that," Luke answered.

Angelina fanned her face with one hand. "That is so romantic. I could jus' die." She sighed dramatically.

"But what about you?" Tessa asked "You're here with Guy? What's up with that? Are you a couple?"

"Yes. I told you he jus' needed to find the right woman." Angelina tossed her glossy brown locks. "I have him right where I want him."

"Is that so?" Guy walked up behind her. "I think it is I who have captured you, *chérie.*" He pulled her in for a long kiss.

When he released her she batted at him playfully. "Guy! Not here. We're in a church!"

He laughed wickedly. "Then we should find somewhere... more private. *Non?*"

She giggled and allowed him to lead her toward the door.

Luke pulled Tessa down to sit on his lap. They watched as one by one, the majority of the people left for home.

I can't believe these people were okay with me marrying you," she whispered, laying her cheek on his head.

"Why?"

"Well. You know..."

"Let me tell you something. The head deacon? He used to be an enforcer for a gang. He beat people up if they didn't pay up. The youth leader? He use to get high all the time and only came to church because he wanted to see how many virgins he could bed. I could go on. Everyone here has a past. They're all different people now. No one is going to judge you for your past."

"But how are we going to pay them back? They let you have fifty grand."

"I'm going to put my mountain bike up for sale. I should be able to get five or six thousand for it. I've already told Delores to cut my salary back. Things will be tight for a while but we'll manage. Then, of course we'll save more money when you can give up your basement suite and move in with me," Luke said.

"We can put my whole salary to paying back the church." Tessa smiled down at him and kissed him. "I can even pick up some shifts from Big Joe."

"No!" Luke looked horrified.

Tessa laughed. "I mean as a waitress, silly."

"Oh." He thought a moment. "How about extra shifts at the hotel instead?"

"Fine. At the hotel then." She kissed his forehead. "It's a shame though. I have all these dance moves I'll never be able to use again."

"That is a shame." He gave her a little squeeze. "We can't let all those moves go to waste. I guess you'll just have to save them for me."

"*Pastor Luke!*" She pretended to look scandalized .

"After we're married of course." He grinned up at her.

Tessa laughed. "I do love you."

"I love you more, my little angel."

# THE END

# BOOKS IN THE THURSTON HOTEL SERIES

http://www.thurstonhotelbooks.com/

A Thurston Promise, Book1
By Brenda Sinclair

Opposite of Frozen, Book 2
By Jan O'Hara

On a Whim, Book 3
By Win Day

Love Under Construction, Book 4
By Sheila Seabrook

A Lasting Harmony, Book 5
By Shelley Kassian

With Open Arms, Book 6
By M. K. Stelmack


The Starlight Garden, Book 7
By Maeve Buchanan


Betting on Courage, Book 8
By Alyssa Linn Palmer


The Thurston Heirloom, Book 9
By Suzanne Stengl


An Angel's Secret, Book 10
By Ellen Jorgy


To a Tea, Book 11
By Katie O'Connor


A Thurston Christmas, Book 12
By Brenda Sinclair

# About The Author

Ellen Jorgy lives in Central Alberta with her husband, Bob, and two children, on a ten acre property with a menagerie of creatures both large and small. She works by day as a Medical Ultrasound Technologist, and by night as an unpaid taxi driver for her children. Somewhere in the midst of all that she finds time to write.

*An Angel's Secret* is her first published work of fiction.

## You can find Ellen at:

Website: *www.ellenjorgy.com*

Facebook @ellenjorg2